Faith
In
What?

Faith
In
What?

a novel
by

Richard
Krawiec

Avisson Press, Inc.
Greensboro 1996

Faith In What?

First Edition.
Printed in the United States of America.
ISBN 1-888105-05-4
Library of Congress Catalog Card Number 95-81791

A portion of this book, in different form, first appeared in *Shenandoah.*

Publisher's Cataloging in Publication

Krawiec, Richard.
      Faith in what? : a novel / by Richard Krawiec.
      p. cm.
      LCCN 95-81791
      ISBN 1-888105-05-4

      I. Title

PS3561.R39F3584 1996   813'.52
                                 QBI96-20039

To Jodi and her mom, who taught me about love, perserverance, and family. And I'd like to thank the Washington Street Writers Group for helping me, in ways they will never know, through the darkest period in my own life. Also Abby, Becky, and Sharon for their friendship and support, and George, in whose apartment I wrote much of this book. Most of all, I'd like to thank God for blessing me with two sons, David and Danny, who have brought me more joy than I could ever have imagined.

Once, in the 1980s...

KATIE WAS SIX years old when it happened. School had been canceled because of the snowstorm, and Katie'd been moping around all day, not knowing what to do with herself. She was driving me nuts. Around two o'clock I finally told her, "That's it, you're going out." It was snowing like crazy, but I figured I could keep an eye on her in the back yard.

"Mumma, I don't want to," she whined.

"Don't start, or you'll be sorry," I told her. "Now get, or I'll spank your heinie." Ellen, who'd been cranky since she woke up in the morning, was finally asleep in the crib in the living room. Timmy wouldn't be home for a couple more hours. I was thinking how those might be the only few minutes of peace I'd have all day.

I pulled the kabob stuff for that night's supper out of the refrigerator. While I skewered the beef and onions and peppers over the sink, I watched out the window as Katie plunked herself right down in a snow drift. She sat there, her back to me, her arms crossed defiantly.

"Oooo, you're so bad sometimes," I said, knowing her pants would be soaked through in no time.

It wasn't more than twenty minutes before she was banging on the door, wanting to be let in.

"What did I tell you?" I said, pulling her inside.

She leaned against the wall and started whining again. I

5

was afraid she was going to wake the baby, so I rinsed my hands, dried them on a towel, and gave Katie a whack on the bum. "There, now you've got something to cry about."

"I don't feel good, Mumma," she said. I looked at her closely and noticed her face was flushed and puffy. When I put my hand to her forehead, the heat of her skin shocked me. "Get up to bed, honey, I'll be right there," I said. Then I called the doctor.

From where the phone was on the end table beside the couch in the front room, I could look out beyond our porch—we rent the middle apartment in a five-unit rowhouse—and see the snow collecting, already starting to drift. I wondered if Timmy would have to leave his car at the plant and walk home. Our street was never plowed, no matter how many times we called to complain. I looked at the snow on the front steps, several inches deep already, and knew I should shovel before it got worse.

The doctor couldn't come. "Of course," he said. "Look outside."

"I am looking," I told him.

"Well, you know then."

"I've got a sick kid. For the goddamn money you make you could rent a snowplow to get you here."

"Mrs..." he hesitated for a moment, forgetting who I was. He told me to give her juice, give her aspirin, call back in the morning if there was any significant change. "It's probably just a virus."

As I hung up, I saw Timmy pull in. His car plowed and skidded to a halt against the back bumper of Shirley's Dodge Dart across the street. The rear end of our Ford pointed out at an angle. Timmy didn't even try to move it, to park it better. He stepped into the road and slammed the door. He's so small, 5'1" and skinny, that he can still buy all his clothes in the teenager's section in Zayre's. But he insists on buying in the Men's Department, so everything is just a little too big on him. Watching him that day, seeing his baggy denim jacket and pants, he looked like a little kid who had dressed up to pretend he was an adult. I might've laughed

6

if I hadn't seen his expression.

He had a beard back then, and the bill of his Pirates' cap hid his eyes. But you could still see that his face was drawn, haggard-looking. His mouth was open wide, like there was a knife in his belly he couldn't pull out.

There were two weeks to go until Christmas. We'd heard the rumors about lay-offs. I just couldn't deal with it right then. So I hurried to the refrigerator, poured a glass of orange juice, and ran up the stairs to Katie's room.

She was laying on top of her bedspread with all her clothes on. Already, a big, round circle of wetness surrounded her black, rubber boots.

"Jesus," I said. I set the glass down on her night table and began to unbuckle them. The rubber felt cold and spongey, like my mother's skin at her wake. A shiver run up my back, but I shook it off. "Just because you're sick, that don't mean you can get away with murder," I told Katie. I yanked her boot off. Her leg was loose. It fell from my hands without resistance. "Hey?" I said. "Hey?"

Then I got that tight feeling in my chest, like the feeling you get when you're washing dishes, and your hand's inside a glass, and the glass cracks and there's no way you can escape your own blame. I looked at Katie's face and her eyes snapped open and her pupils rolled up. I took her frozen hands and shook them. Then I reached up and shook her by the shoulders. I was still shaking her and screaming her name when Timmy came into the room and touched me, his fingers on my neck like ice.

Chapter 1

I HATE THE WAY I've come to think of my youngest daughter, Ellen, as my 'normal' daughter. She doesn't say much about her sister, Katie, but I know Ellen is affected in ways she thinks I'm not aware of. In ways she's not aware of. We all are.

Just today, after coming home from picking up some smile stickers for Katie's progress chart, I was looking through my pocketbook for the door key when I heard Shirley across the street say to a group of neighborhood kids hanging around on her porch, "I wouldn't go over there. Her daughter's got a brain disease."

"You got something to say, spit it out," I said, turning to look at her. She glanced at me, dragged on her cigarette, and pushed her bottom lip forward to exhale. As the smoke floated in a gray triangle towards the bottom of the second-story porch, it seemed to be rising from the purple paisley kerchief on her head. "And it ain't a disease," I muttered, turning back to my door.

"They don't know what it is. For all they know, it could be something like AIDS."

I stopped with the key in the lock, the door just pushed open. The stale air of our house came out like a dog, something faithful, to greet me. "Stop saying that," I spoke loudly, still facing the open doorway. "It ain't a *disease*." My jaw tightened as if it might break. I thought of those kids over there. When Ellen was their age, and Katie too, before they were old enough for school, my porch was the one that was always full. The women in the neighborhood used to push their kids over in their strollers. We'd sit and gab and the porch would be full of babies and toddlers. If it was hot, we'd go out back so the kids could play in the shade of our back yard. After Katie's illness, no one stopped by. Except Shirley, which is what made it so hard listening to her now.

"Yeah," I heard Shirley telling them. "She lets all these strangers into her house. She begs them to come in and do her work for her, for nothing. And she don't even warn 'em."

I'd had it. I tossed the paper bag with the smile stickers into my living room and spun around. Behind me, I heard my husband, Timmy, stir from the couch. He'd been sitting there, listening, the whole time. "Pat?" he called, his voice tired, defeated. But I hurried down our cement steps and across the street without taking my eyes off Shirley. At the foot of her stairs, I looked up and told her, my mouth so tense it barely moved, "It ain't a disease. And I wouldn't have to beg from strangers if friends helped."

She glared down at me from where she sat on her porch railing. "Friends?" Smoke flowed out of her nostrils. The kids shuffled nervously to get behind her. "You might have some friends if you didn't rat on people."

I felt the blood leave my face like my throat had just been slit. I couldn't look at her. When I turned, Timmy was watching from behind the storm door of our rowhouse. He still had his blue Star Wars pajamas on. The sun seemed hot all of a sudden, in a draining sort of way, the air thick and hard to walk through, as if this were one of those muggy summer days. But it was November.

I edged sideways between two cars, barely able to squeeze between them. My knee started acting up; I thought it might give out on me and I'd fall on my face in the street. Not now God, please, I thought. I've had enough. Don't let me embarrass myself any more.

Timmy held the door for me. "Pat, why do you bother?"

he said. "Shirley's Shirley. Let it go and she'll get over it. You know." He started to put his arm around my shoulders. I know he was just trying to help, but this jolt of meanness went through my heart. I shrugged away from him and said, "Why aren't you dressed? It's 11:30."

He tried to joke, "It's my day off."

"Every day is your day off," I snapped.

"This is my unemployment day."

"You don't have to be there 'til one. If you didn't spend so much time sitting on your ass, maybe you'd find something." I knew that wasn't fair—he had been looking for work. I knew I'd hurt him. As he turned to go up the stairs to the bedroom to change, I wanted to apologize. But I couldn't bring myself to say, "I'm sorry."

I looked back out, across the street at Shirley. She was staring back, and when she saw me, she made a motion with her hand, for me to come over. Kind of an apologizing motion. "Screw you," I said. I slammed the door and leaned my back against the wood, thinking, Why do I say these things?

We used to be close, me and Timmy, and Shirley and her Jim. Bowling every Wednesday, cookouts, Steelers games. We'd take turns giving each other a break—some days I'd watch Jimmy Jr., who was a year older than Ellen. Other days, Shirley would take Ellen and Katie. We were real friendly before Katie got sick, and all the time she was still in the hospital. I can't remember how many times we came home from visiting Katie to find a casserole all made, waiting for us. And, of course, Shirley was always looking after Ellen.

Once we brought Katie home, it was a different story. Shirley still called me every day, or yelled across the street if she saw me sitting on my porch. But every time I asked her over, she had an excuse ready for why she couldn't come, then why Jimmy Jr. couldn't visit. Once I went over there, but she was so nervous. She leaned away from me and breathed slowly, out the side of her mouth. After I left, I watched from behind the drapes of my front window as she went inside her house and came back out wearing those yellow Playtex gloves, carrying a rag and a bottle of Mr. Clean. She spent five minutes scrubbing down the chair where I'd been sitting. I knew she was just doing it, she was worried for her kids. That didn't stop it from hurting, though.

I spoke to her on the phone after that. Until last week, when she called to tell me how to lie—how to make up a fake lease to get housing assistance, how to pretend me and Timmy were separated so I could get DPA and Medical. I told her, "I ain't listening. I don't wanna hear it. I got my pride. I ain't gonna lie."

"You're lying to yourself every day," she said. "Face it. Katie's a vegetable. If you're not going to send her away, at least make it work for you."

I was ripshit. I slammed down the receiver and, I was so mad, without even thinking I called up the people downtown. "I want to report a fraud," I said. "There's someone on my street who's pretending that they're renting out a room to someone on public assistance so you guys will weatherize their house for free." I gave them Shirley and Jim's name and address and hung up. I tried to call back, the next day, to cancel it. But it was too late.

I admit, I was wrong. I wish I hadn't called. People do what they think they have to; Shirley and Jim have their needs, too. Knowing it was my fault they'll probably have to pay a fine, see their names in the paper, I can see her hating me. I accept that.

Still, she's got no right to make things hard for Ellen, turn all the kids in the neighborhood against her. I know Ellen walks home alone every day. Even at six years old, though, she's too proud to let me pick her up at school. She doesn't want me to know what's going on.

But I do know. And it breaks my heart.

There are times when I feel like standing on my porch and screaming at the top of my lungs for everyone to hear, "Nail me if you want, but just leave my girls the hell alone."

Chapter 2

THE LAST THING he needed, Timmy thought, was Pat yelling at him again. What ever happened to helping each other out? Giving each other a little support. Yeah, sure, it'd been a long time since he'd brought home a paycheck. But he was the one that was out of work. Didn't she understand what that meant to him? It was like his whole point of being alive was gone. Things hadn't changed in the same way for her. She had always been home with the kids. She hadn't lost nothing. If anything, what she did was even more important than ever. Although, to be truthful about it, Timmy thought she was going overboard with Katie. Everything was Katie this and Katie that. Katie Katie Katie. What about the rest of them?

As if in punishment for his thoughts, the car stalled out midway through an intersection. "Damn me," Timmy yelled, banging his hand on the steering wheel. He turned the key and the engine didn't even crank. Great, great, he thought. This is the last straw. Last straw for what? he wondered. Before he could consider the question, though, the horns were already starting to beep behind him.

It was his own fault. The car had been bucking and stalling for several weeks, but Timmy hadn't bothered to lift the hood. Even if they had the money to fix it, he knew nothing about cars. He'd made it a point not to learn about them back in high school, when his old man got on his case about it. "Every guy in this city knows how to take care of their car," his father had said. "What are you, some kind of faggot? Afraid to get a little grease on your hands?"

They were at the supper table—they were always at the supper table when his father started these arguments—and Timmy had been trying to ignore it, like his mother did. She was humming to herself, busily passing the potatoes and chicken around. But his father kept on about Timmy being a faggot, a sissy, until Timmy finally banged the serving bowl which held the mashed potatoes onto the tabletop.

"Why should I even try to learn? It'd only give you something else to criticize. You don't like nothing about me. I'm too short for basketball, too slow for football, too weak for the mill, too dumb for college, my girlfriend is a fat pig." He looked at his mother for support. She kept her head down, absorbed in the act of tucking a pat of butter inside the hole she'd made for it in the top of her mound of potatoes.

His father, a heavy-chested man with forearms so large they seemed swollen, leaned across the table. His face, naturally pink, looked dark from the grit which was embedded in his skin. His eyes were small and grey and held the same piercing, focused look, the look of intense, yet limited, concentration, found in the eyes of a guard dog. He told Timmy, "What do you want me to do, apologize for your life?"

At that moment Timmy swore he would never again try to learn anything that his father wanted him to know.

But now, as he sat, unmoving, watching the light change from green to red and back to green, trying to ignore the horns beeping behind him, the angry looks and fingers from those people in the cars which pulled out and veered around him, Timmy wished he hadn't been so stubborn. Sure, the old man had been a jerk. Still, if Timmy could've forgiven him, he'd have that information now. He would've learned something he could use.

The engine finally turned over, caught. He revved it up, dropped the column shift into Drive. The car jerked forward, hesitated, but he stomped on the gas pedal and it surged ahead.

He noticed the light was red as he ran through it. To his right, brakes squealed, a horn blared, but he didn't turn. He didn't want to know how close he'd come.

Learned something, he repeated to himself as he headed south out of his neighborhood, past the two engine fire station, the convenience store, and the Catholic church, separated from the town by the small hill it sat atop and the dark moat of its parking lot. He was beginning to feel he had nothing to offer anyone; there was nothing he could do; there was no place where he fit. What was supposed to happen to guys like him?

Pat wasn't helping much either, he told himself. She was right, and she was wrong. Yeah, maybe he should've been out looking for jobs. But she'd never spent a year and a half pounding the pavement only to have everyone tell you you didn't have the 'right' skills. There were only so many times you could be told you weren't good enough. After a while, you couldn't put yourself in a position to hear it; not if you wanted to be able to look in a mirror and tell yourself you had some value, you were still a man. For whatever the hell that was worth, Timmy thought.

He wheeled into a parking lot before a small plaza and took a ticket from an elderly black man trying to stay warm in a plywood booth barely large enough to fit a stool inside. Timmy resented having to pay for parking. It was only a dollar, but it didn't seem right to have to pay to pick up your unemployment check. People on welfare got theirs mailed to them. Was he any worse?

He sat inside the car, feeling his tension build. By the time he decided to go ahead in, it felt like his insides were full of twisted bands and too-tight gears. Every step closer seemed to twist him tighter. It was as if the ground contained invisible cranks which connected immediately with the soles of his work boots each time one of his feet touched down; whenever he shifted his weight onto his toes, the crank was heaved another turn, tightening the hidden cords which ran from his feet to his head. The tension slithered upwards with the rippling, muscular movement of a snake. When it reached the top of his spine, instead of a release, it gathered in such an increasingly large knot that Timmy felt his skull would not be able to contain it. He wished he could just cut into his head with a knife to release it.

Oh, man, everything, he thought. Pat, Katie, Ellen, this hot day, the city itself—it was all conspiring against him. Even this dumpy plaza. He looked at the unemployment office sandwiched between a liquor store and a laundromat. Beside the liquor store was an empty storefront; the sight of its soaped-up windows filled Timmy with a surprising perk of rage. Why did they have to put the unemployment office here, in this part of town? Mostly blacks lived here, and most of the people collecting were white. This is Pittsburgh, Timmy thought. In this city, blacks weren't able to get jobs in the first place, so of course they wouldn't be collecting unemployment.

Timmy pulled open the glass door and stepped into an oblong room. The light glaring down from the overhead fluorescent tubes filled the space with a harsh, unnatural brightness which hit him with an almost physical force. It was like he'd been slapped in the forehead so hard that his eyeballs had popped forward in their sockets. He felt humiliated. Here he was, begging. On the dole. He remembered his father telling him once, "Real men can always find work."

Timmy ducked his head involuntarily, even as his eyes sought familiar faces. The newspapers and TV had been full lately of sob stories about all the unemployed yuppies, people who'd lost their sixty and seventy thousand dollar a year jobs. As he settled into line behind the twenty or so people ahead of him, Timmy wondered why the hell the newspaper and TV people weren't here, at this office. He sure as hell hadn't seen many stories about these people right here. None of them had ever made sixty grand in a year. Did that mean their lives didn't matter?

Someone coughed. Timmy looked around, frightened. He wondered if he'd been talking out loud again. Betty Lane, a tall, lanky, black woman who'd been released from her nurse's aide job after 15 years when her hospital decided to replace most of the staff with permanent, part-time workers, gave him a small, sad smile. Michael Wurster, a compact, round-faced man half-winked his eyes and nodded his head, as if to say, Hold on. Hold on yourself, Timmy felt like telling him. Michael, who'd been a clerk downtown before the latest city cutbacks, had taken to wearing loose sweatshirts, dungarees, sandals, and a chin beard that reminded Timmy of Maynard G. Krebs. He was enrolled in some sort of job training that included a poet.

To Timmy, poetry, ballet—it was all the same. The guys who did that stuff probably wore bikini underpants and shaved their legs and he just didn't want to get too close to them.

Timmy looked along the line. There weren't too many guys from the plant still coming. A number had moved away. Those who were left seemed too embarrassed to look at you now. There were all kinds of new people, and they didn't want to look at the old-timers either, as if they feared bad luck was contagious. Old-timer, Timmy thought. This is what I got my experience at now. Collecting. Standing in line. But for how much longer? Timmy was into his extended benefits, and when they ran out? What would happen then? Why wasn't anybody talking about that? Thinking about it, he guessed Jim was right after all.

The last time Timmy had seen his best friend, was two days before Pat called up to report Jim and Shirley. Timmy didn't know how he'd ever be able to look Jim in the face again, but that was another story.

Then, a bunch of guys had gone to Harry's Tavern to watch the football games. At halftime, the conversation got away from football. Everyone started complaining about all the news stories saying how great Pittsburgh was—the #1 City, Best Place to Live. Best for who? they wanted to know. How could you figure #1 when so many guys were out of work?

"But you're not real," Jim told those circled behind him where he sat at the bar. Jim was a lanky man, with tight red curls and bushy eyebrows. He looked thin, except his arms were so thick the guys called him Popeye. Whenever he was at the bar, people crowded around him, and Timmy felt lucky to be his friend. Jim was funny and smart—he'd gone to Pitt for two years before dropping out. Timmy had asked him once why he hadn't finished, and Jim told him that he liked hanging out with the guys. If he went to college, he'd have to get new friends.

"The thing is," Jim had told the guys at Harry's, "people don't see us anymore. Guys like us are fine if we're statues they can put up and moon over. But us here—the real us—we're an embarrassment. You know? We're the cavemen who crashed the cocktail party. We're a pain in the ass. They look at us and say, You still here? We give Pittsburgh a bad name. We expect to get *paid* for working. We *refuse* to kiss ass for a job. So they write us off, pretend we aren't here. If they pretend hard enough, they can convince these other corporations that they don't have to see us, that they can pretend, too, that we're extinct. How do you think they got all these business headquarters to move in downtown?"

Timmy remembered this as he looked around at the people standing quietly in line at unemployment. They slouched, or stood hunched over, heads down. Lined up like bad children waiting to be punished. For what? Needing to make a living? Not having work? Being alive?

Inside him, the tension was winding tighter. Did Pat think he liked doing this? Standing until his legs got tired, shuffling forward an inch or two every few minutes? He looked at the I.D. in his hand, his picture like the photo of a convict—that same haunted, exhausted look to the eyes, the mouth downturned. She didn't have any idea how it felt to be here. To see the way the woman behind the counter looked at you when you passed your I.D. forward and she, in return, gave you a check; her eyes and mouth so severe with judgement it made you feel like a worthless parasite, so you couldn't even enjoy the pleasure of the money they gave you, the little money, not enough, never enough.

A baby started crying and the sound surprised Timmy. He became aware that the line had stalled. As he looked around those before him, towards the counter, he became aware that his face was covered with sweat, and that surprised him, too. He swabbed at the sweat with a handkerchief and checked his watch.

He'd been there twenty minutes already. The baby cried louder, and he saw, at the front of the line, a young, long-haired woman rocking side to side in an effort to calm her child. No one was behind the counter.

The two women who were supposed to be working the line stood at the rear of the office, at the desk of their supervisor. He was a tall man with small, weasel-like eyes, only pale and colorless, and thick, white blonde hair that fell in a boyish bang to cover half his forehead. The three of them were drinking soda, laughing and sharing a chocolate birthday cake. It was apparently the supervisor's birthday.

Softly, the people in line began to complain, muttering about the break being too long, and people partying while they were there needing money to pay their bills. One man said, "I have a job interview." An elderly woman with a cane said, "I got varicose veins." She looked around for someplace to sit, couldn't find a chair, and started searching the floor, as if trying to find a section of linoleum that wasn't filmy with dirt.

The baby was wailing now, arching backwards in its mother's arms. The mother swayed and bounced the baby, switched the child from hip to hip, cooed, "I know, I know, you been patient honey, I know, I know." It didn't help. She told the line, "He's hungry." The way she tipped her head, it was apparent the baby was still breast-feeding. "I don't want to lose my place," she said. "I'm next. If they ever get back here."

A grumbled assent grew in volume like a wave peaking. At the supervisor's desk, the two women pointedly turned their backs to those waiting at the front.

The baby's cry grew louder, more distressed. Timmy felt a clutch in his chest. He remembered when Katie and Ellen were that small, how agonizing it had been to listen to their sorrow those times when he could find no way to comfort them. He looked at the mother and child. It wasn't right. Didn't the people who worked here at least care about kids? Before he knew he was speaking, he was calling out, "Hey, we got babies here, old people, and, you know, we busted our asses, too. What, do we have to call that disc jockey Wayne Van Dine on KDKA to get our checks?"

There were murmurs of agreement and one loud clap. Timmy, encouraged, shouted, "We don't need this crap from you lazy bastards."

At the rear of the office, the women turned frontward. The man, his hands to the desk, rose. All three focused their eyes forward as if shooting lasers.

Everyone in line, it seemed, looked away, shuffled to one side or the other. Timmy could swear he heard someone whimper. He found himself alone, in an open space, facing the visible hatred of those who worked there.

The women came forward and processed the people through without a word. When it was Timmy's turn, he passed his I.D. card across the counter to a woman in her late thirties. Her eyebrows were thick and dark and rose dramatically when she spoke. Her hair had been dyed an orangey blonde, and cut short all around with a flamelike tuft left on top. Her lips, painted with lipstick slightly darker than her hair, looked too thin for her full square jaw.

Timmy wanted to apologize. "It's just...you know...it's like, nobody's hiring...and when you're used to work-ing...sometimes..."

"My ex worked at a mill," she said, nailing him with her hard, brown eyes. "He told me all about slowing down, so the job would go into overtime. One Memorial Day, him and his buddies pulled out cots and slept for eight hours. At double time and a half. He got laid off and thought he was going to pull the same crap on me. So don't tell me about busting your ass."

Timmy looked down at his hands. He wanted to tell her he didn't work at a mill, that her ex was only one guy. But he was afraid to speak.

"I put in forty hours a week here," she said, "and I am sick of hearing you people whine as if you're the only ones who ever lost a job." She turned and called to the supervisor, "Mr. Kingchester." She put Timmy's file aside and ordered him to move over and wait.

"For what?" he asked.

She looked past him. "Next."

Mr. Kingchester sat, chair tipped back, his feet crossed at the ankles and propped on the corner of his desk. He smiled at Timmy for a while before moving slowly to the front to retrieve Timmy's file. Returning to his desk, he resumed his position with Timmy's file open in his lap. After examining his fingernails, Mr. Kingchester took out a pair of clippers and laboriously worked on trimming them.

Timmy turned around, paced. He felt like everyone was watching him. He didn't know what to do, what to say. The people in line moved forward, got their checks, moved on. Mr. Kingchester rose slowly, stretched, sauntered to the coffee machine, where he chatted with another man for several minutes. When he returned to his desk, he sipped from a heavy, white mug, looked at Timmy's file again. He jotted some notes down on a pad, then made a phone call. Finally, he disappeared into the men's room.

Timmy went to the counter to complain but the woman, before he could speak, told him, "Step aside, we have others to process."

Mr. Kingchester returned, tucked Timmy's file into a vertical plastic holder on his deck, and came casually forward, his hands in the pockets of his pants. His jacket was pushed back by his arms so that it looked like there were tweed wings at his hips. "No check today," he said.

"What are you talking about?" Timmy looked up, feeling intimidated, like he always did when he had to ask something of anyone taller than him.

The man's colorless lips moved into a false, reptilian smile. "We have to check a few things."

"What things? I been coming here for..."

"Possible fraud," the man said, cutting Timmy off. He turned and started whistling "Happy Days Are Here Again," as he walked off.

Chapter 3

TODAY when Ellen came home, she was flustered in the way you expect someone who's a mother to be flustered. She almost looked like she wasn't a kid anymore. Her hands were on the hips of her green plaid skirt and her mouth was open in outrage. A dark space showed where her front tooth was missing.

I felt like grabbing her up and hugging her until she had no breath left. But I hadn't hugged her since this whole thing with Katie began. I was afraid to.

"I'm not going back to that creepy school," Ellen said.

From where I was, in the middle of the cellar, looking up, it seemed like the rough ceiling beam beside the staircase cut her head off just above her thick, black eyebrows. "What now?" I asked her. "What's the matter?" First grade, I thought. God help me.

Ellen looked at the volunteers holding hands in a circle around the table Katie was stretched upon. Ellen took a step up, back towards the kitchen. Who could blame her?

These guys, my Monday group, all come from a small Evangelical church run out of somebody's house. They scare me, the way they pray like they're waiting to cash in, like they've just bought lottery tickets. But what can I do? I need sixty volunteers a week to run Katie through her 'patterning' program, but I'm lucky to get half that. I can't afford to be choosey.

In the three years Katie's been home from the hospital, volunteers have come and gone week by week. In that time, I've had my share of weirdos—guys who wanted to put her on a rice diet, others who insisted she exercise under different-colored lights. One girl thought listening to whale songs might help.

But these people with their prayers bothered me the most. They wouldn't quit. When it didn't work, they blamed it on me, saying I wasn't concentrating. I didn't know if they were crazy, or if they'd hit the nail right on the head. When you're desperate, you'll grab at anything.

Their leader, John, is a bent, gaunt man, all angled, like his bones are pipe cleaners someone has twisted into the form of a person, but hasn't been able to quite straighten out. With his thin face and heavy, brown-framed glasses, he looks like an insect. He gazed at Ellen like he wanted to hypnotize her or something, and said, "Come pray with us. God wants you down here right now. Don't you love your sister?" His Adam's apple rose and fell like an elevator.

Ellen scuffed a cloud of dust off the wooden stairs with her shiny black shoes. Plastic, all we could afford, but if you didn't look too close you might think they were patent leather.

"You don't have to if you don't want to," I told her.

"You're fighting us," John told me. "You're fighting God's plan. This could be our big breakthrough."

Linda, a middle-aged woman with short red hair so bluntly cut it looks like her hairdresser uses a steak knife, rolled her eyes. "Pat," she said. She wore a wooden cross the size of a model airplane around her neck, and she raised this towards me. "You got to get your act together. The Lord's not going to let your child come back into a messed-up home."

"You have to have faith in us," John lectured. "God wants us to heal her, so the world will have to listen to what we have to say. But you're preventing us."

I didn't know. What if they were right? What if it was my fault Katie wasn't getting better, just like it'd been my fault she got sick in the first place? I looked at the group, holding hands as they stood in a circle around the exercise table where Katie lay. I stepped forward, to break in and join them. Both hands I took were damp and cold. "Get down here," I yelled back at Ellen. She closed her mouth, blew air out of her nostrils, turned her face away and started tapping one foot.

All around me the volunteers, following John's example, began speaking in religious phrases; Lord this and Lord that, glory and beseech and mercy. I looked at Katie, her long body stretched on the vinyl-topped work table. Though her muscle tone was good from all the exercises we put her through, her face was slack. Her teeth angled out in all directions and her eyes slanted so that she looked Chinese. No one had figured out, yet, how to exercise face muscles. She made sucking motions with her mouth and stared up at the ceiling. Her pupils were a shallow, solid brown that reflected all light. They never focused on anything, but my new doctor claimed she wasn't blind. Sometimes, I just wanted to poke her eyes, to get her attention. Imagining it, I could see my finger bouncing on the surface of her pupil. Without realizing I was speaking out loud, I said, "Come on now, cut the crap, it's been long enough. What more do you want from me? Jesus, I'm sorry."

The people in the circle stopped swaying. Tension flowed like currents from their hands into mine. "Amen," I said. "Amen amen amen."

John slowly began again. "Lord, please help these sinners..."

I closed my eyes. I wanted Katie to walk again, and I didn't care if it was magic, or if I had to cut my arm off to do it. The three years I'd been working with Katie since she'd come back from the hospital seemed like ninety. It was hard for me to remember what she'd been like when she was normal. There were times, at the end of the day, when I sat down alone to rest, that I couldn't remember the first thing about how life used to be. Even my home—the den, the kitchen, the bedroom—seemed alien, like another world. The only place I felt comfortable was in the cellar; the only thing real was Katie's exercise program. The only solid people in my life were the volunteers. At those times, when I thought about Ellen and Timmy, they seemed like ghosts.

If I sat long enough thinking, I'd begin to hate everything about my life. I was so ashamed of feeling that way, I couldn't talk to anyone about it. But I was sick of the whole kit and caboodle.

I was sick of having to tell everyone my problems, of having to beg for help. Every month I have to xerox these flyers —across the top, KATIE'S GONNA WIN is written above the drawing I did of her face, tracing it from her first-grade photo. Beneath that is the short explanation of her brain damage and the help I need.

I was sick of tacking these flyers to telephone poles, taping them in store windows, arguing with priests that they should let me stack them in the backs of churches. I was sick of seeing my daughter's face everywhere I went, then sitting home and hoping somebody, anybody, would call to volunteer.

I was sick, too, of holding spoons to Katie's mouth, having to feed her, clean her off, sit her up, set her down, dress and undress this eleven-year-old person who's more helpless than any baby.

I was sick of playing with her, reading to her, getting no response. Of changing diapers, cleaning her adult mess. I was sick of seeing no change, no improvement, nothing.

I'd been losing faith that she was going to get better, and I hated myself for that. In church all the time they told us you just had to have faith and everything would work out. But the priests never talked much about what to do when you found yourself losing faith. And I could never figure out what I was supposed to have faith in anyways. I wanted Katie to get better, so we could be a regular, happy family again, with our own normal problems. But what if God didn't want her to get better? What if Katie didn't? Nobody wants to think about these things, but once they get in your head, you can't stop it. I was getting so, I didn't know what to hope for anymore. "Katie," I said now, "Please. For Mumma."

She opened her mouth. Spit drooled out the side. She struggled to lift her right arm, her good arm, towards her face, so she could suck on the cramped fingers of that hand.

"No," I said. I broke free of the circle and pulled her hand away, slapped it lightly. "How many times have I told you not to do that?" Behind me, the circle whisked closer. Someone brushed against me and that gave me the creeps. John, his voice shaky and bouncing, said, "Let this child walk, Lord."

"Please, Katie, please," I whispered, stroking her thick, rough hair. I pushed it back behind her ears. "You little jerk. Don't be defiant. Do something. Say something. Say Mumma. Just say Mumma."

"Mumma," Ellen said from the stairs. "Don't you want to hear what happened?"

I had forgotten she was there. "Not now," I said crossly, without turning. "Why don't you just wash your hands and get down here and help me."

"You never help *me*," she said, and I heard her quick, stomping footsteps on the stairs. The sound of the door slamming made my heart feel like someone had suddenly squeezed it.

Even if I hadn't been afraid, I wouldn't have been able to go up to her. Because Katie had a startle-reaction, a mini-seizure, right then. It was her third of the week. Watching her, it felt like the air suddenly evaporated from my lungs. I leaned back as her body jerked, grew rigid. Her arms and legs, pulled by their tightening muscles, rose and crossed before her. For the few seconds the seizure lasted, Katie's face looked pained and confused. Then, slowly, as her muscles relaxed and her limbs lowered to the table, she let out a soft, animal purr that sounded like a laugh. Her eyes grew distant and glossy. They didn't even look like eyes, but like windows opening to another world.

Katie was in the Rehabilitation Hospital for nearly two years. Over a dozen specialists saw her, ran hundreds of tests, but no one could ever figure out what happened, what caused the seizure which left her brain-damaged. I thought it was pretty suspicious that the doctors decided to turn her out of the hospital just as our insurance benefits ran dry. Bunch of thieves, I thought. You trust these people to take care of you, but all they do is take you for a ride. I mean, they give you this song and dance about caring, but if you add up all the volunteers I had helping me, they wouldn't make the money one doctor does. But do you ever see a doctor giving his time for nothing?

The day they kicked us out of the hospital, the doctors tried to convince us to dump Katie into a state insitution. They told us it was the best thing for everyone; her brain damage was permanent, irreversible. They could transfer her directly. All we'd have to do was sign the papers, and we could just go home. But me and Timmy, we wouldn't go for it.

"I don't care what you say," I told the main doctor on her case, Dr. Tom Flaherty, a short, tubby man with large hands who for some reason reminded me of a lobster. "I'm not quitting on her. She's family. I know she's going to get better."

"It's not a matter of quitting. It's a matter of being realistic." He spoke in a superior tone, like he was explaining something to a dim-witted child. "We've run every test, tried every procedure..."

"I don't care about your tests and your procedures," I told him. "I can feel it in my heart."

He smirked, making no effort to hide it. His nose twitched, and he shook his head sympathetically at Timmy, who looked away.

"You think you're so Goddamn smart," I said. "Well answer me this—how come you can't even tell us what the hell happened to her?"

"Pat," Timmy said. Katie was only eight then, not so big as she is now. Timmy had her cradled in his arms because they wouldn't even let us keep the wheelchair. He reached out two fingers from the hand supporting Katie's legs, opening the fingers like scissor blades, trying to grab me. I stepped aside. I was fuming, I was so mad.

"It was some type of neurological event," Dr. Flaherty said. He wiped his forehead with a tissue from the pocket of his lab coat. His skin was splotchy, like someone who's never done any physical work in their life.

"Well you can take your *event* and shove it," I said.

Timmy stepped close and grabbed my blouse sleeve between his fingers. It was a shiny, fake-satin blouse that I bought for visiting the hospital, but oddly it made me feel less like a woman than the T-shirts I usually wore.

"C'mon Pat, forget it. Let's go," Timmy said.

"No," I said, pulling away. "No. I don't care. Who do these people think they are? She's a little girl, for God's sake, not an animal. I'm not going to put her away. If we were Andrew Carnegie you can bet your ass we wouldn't be treated like this."

"We're not Andrew Carnegie," Timmy said, sounding embarrassed.

I looked at Katie then. At that time, her hair was long, and as her head lolled over Timmy's arm, it hung in a dark curtain towards the floor. Her eyes were skittering back and forth, back and forth.

Though I'd never really thought about God much in my life—to me he was a baby at Christmas time and this bleeding guy nailed to a cross at Easter; and His Father was this white-bearded guy hanging out in the clouds—I prayed then, Dear God, please make her do something and show this asshole that there's still hope.

I touched Katie's face—quicker and harder than I'd intended—and it must've shocked her, because she had one of those startle-reactions, right there. It was the first one I'd ever seen and I was too scared to be hysterical. She gave out a sharp cry and her body went rigid in Timmy's arms. The doctor didn't move; he did nothing.

I watched her relax like something deflating. Her unblinking pupils began to shine, as if a bulb behind them was being raised to a brighter intensity. Her mouth widened into a private grin. I didn't know where she was, but wherever, something there was making her happy.

In that moment, I stared at her without love or heartbreak, with just a blank sorrow, as if I were a witness to the bloodless tragedy of a stranger. In a way, I envied her.

Chapter 4

TIMMY PARKED AT THE CURB in front of Harry's Tavern. It was a low cement building with a door and one long window lit by a yellow neon sign for IRON CITY. The asphalt sidewalk in front of the bar was buckled and cracked, as if moles were pushing tunnels beneath it. The tar was a scuffed-looking white gray. That used to give Timmy a comforting feeling, a sense of security, back when he was working and all the guys would come here after a shift. It was like Harry's had been there forever, and always would be; the men coming to it from work as if attending church. But now...Timmy paused at the door to glance across the street, at the hulking brick plant where he used to work. The metal gates were wrapped with chains and padlocked. It was hard to believe he'd spent one-third of his life working there. Turning back to the bar, Timmy felt small, rundown, empty. Used.

He stepped inside and stopped to let his eyes adjust to the darkness. He was hoping Jim would be there. The idea of meeting Jim agitated Timmy in a good way. It would be like doing something you weren't supposed to, but doing it anyways because you knew no one would catch you. Pat and Shirley wouldn't have to know. It could be their secret, Timmy's and Jim's. It hadn't been that long since the women had had their blow-up, but Timmy already missed Jim. Missed sitting on one of their porches, or tooling around the city in one of their cars, talking or saying nothing. Jim had always been like a big brother to Timmy, someone Timmy could trust to listen and not make fun of what he had to say. Jim was the type of guy who could offer advice without it seeming he was trying to tell you what to do. But Timmy was a little afraid, too. What if Jim were there and didn't want to talk to him? In the past, when Pat and Shirley had their squabbles, Jim stayed out of it. This time, though, it was costing Jim money. That might make things different.

In any case, Jim wasn't there. The place was almost empty. Two heavy-bellied men wearing denim jackets sat in the corner booth. And, at the bar...a black guy? Timmy gaped at the man slouched on a stool halfway down the worn counter. The man's arms rested on the wooden rail as if he'd been there a while, nursing the beer before him. He was an older man with a moustache and gray curls so tight to his scalp they seemed to be clinging there. He was the first black guy Timmy had ever seen in Harry's.

Timmy stepped forward as if hypnotized. He was made nervous by the fact that he didn't know what was the right word to use for this guy. Timmy was comfortable with the term Black, but he'd seen where the newspapers were starting to use African-American. When he was a kid, it was all right to call them coloreds. They used the term themselves. Of course, there was that other word. He remembered the jokes he'd hear from his father, the other men at the mill. How do you babysit a nigger? Lick their lips and stick them to the wall. If a nigger, a Jew, and an Irishman went over a cliff in a Cadillac, who would die first? Who cares, but it's a shame to waste a good car.

Timmy had never told those jokes himself, but he'd listened and laughed. As he took a stool two seats down from the man, he bowed his head, embarassed about that. Since he'd been out of work, he'd been feeling a whole lot less grudging towards a lot of people—people on welfare, guys living on the streets, Blacks. Timmy never believed, like a lot of the guys, that affirmative action was responsible for lost jobs. He knew the guys were just saying that because it gave them someone to blame. But Timmy knew what happened to him had nothing to do with this Black man. This African-American. This whatever the hell he was supposed to call him. He felt frustrated, not knowing the right thing to say. Why couldn't they pick out one word and stick with it, like everybody else? Hunky. Polack. Mick. Kraut. Guinea. It was probably the fault of the damn newspapers. They were the ones who were making a big deal about it, trying to tell him what he was supposed to do and think and say—as if they understood anything about anyone's life.

The man tipped his head in greeting. Timmy mumbled "Hi," but didn't look over. Harry, a white-haired man with Slavic features gone loose so that his cheeks hung below his jaw line, dealt a cocktail napkin to the counter before Timmy. "Get a draft?" Timmy said, pulling a few crumpled dollar bills and assorted coins from his dungarees pocket.

Harry angled a mug under an Iron City tap. While the glass filled he said, "Anyone who pays can get a drink here." His voice was pitched to carry to the men in the corner. There was a disgusted grunt and grumble from the two guys back there. Timmy tossed them a quick look, then turned to his glass.

Harry stepped back, leaned against the shelves and watched a game show on TV.

"My Daddy grew up out here," the man said.

"Yeah, where?" Harry asked.

The man told him the street, but Harry shook his head. He looked at Timmy.

"Never heard of it," Timmy said, looking at the man.

"You wouldn't," the man said, delicately preening his moustache with his thumb and forefinger. "It's on the east side."

"Oh," Harry nodded.

"Back in the days when you had to sweep your porch three times a day to get the grit off."

"I remember," Harry said. Timmy noticed that the two men were about the same age, in their sixties. Despite the obvious differences, there were odd points of similarity. They were both round-bodied, with large arms, weary looking faces. Only Harry's lips were pulled tight, as if he were constipated, while this man's mouth opened into an easy smile.

"At least everybody was working back then. Before the damn environmentalists destroyed the steel industry." Harry folded and unfolded his arms, straightened the gray cloth draped over his apron string.

"Hell, I don't think they were the problem," the man said. He leaned back in his stool, shaking his head. He gave a soft laugh. "When we was growing up, my Daddy told us, 'This country will always need steel, and this city will always need men strong enough to make it. As long as there's a God and a union.'" The man chuckled again, looked at Timmy. The man's eyes were a dusty grayish-blue. "He always said to put your trust in God, but your faith in the union. The old fool."

Timmy watched Harry stiffen, grip the counter behind him. There was a quick shuffling sound from the corner. "What was that?" one of those men said. He came forward, a meaty-faced man with short, sandy hair. He leaned one hand on the bar beside the Black man and said, "You bad-mouthing unions?"

"Sit your ass down," Harry said. The man eased back, but didn't leave.

"You don't think they sold us out, too?" the Black man said.

"Pal," Harry told him, taking the cloth from the thin belt of his apron and setting it on the counter. "All these people out here used to work at that plant." He motioned with his head towards the door.

"Used to." the man said. "Used to. Are your union reps out of work, too?"

There was an edgy silence. "I get your point," Harry said.

"I don't," the man with the sandy hair added. His friend, wearing a salt and pepper beard and moustache and a billed cap was beside him now, his hands in the pockets of his black-and-red checkered jacket.

The old man shook his head, held his hands open. "You know what the problem is with you people?"

Before either of the men behind the Black man could

31

move, Harry shot his right hand straight out, pointing at each in turn. "I won't have trouble in my bar."

"Well tell him," the sandy-haired man said. His face was a dark scarlet. "He's the one running down unions and white people."

"I didn't say nothing bad about no white people."

"What did you just say?" the man demanded.

The man shook his head and laughed. He must be crazy, Timmy thought. These guys would kill him. The man spoke to Harry. "I was saying, the problem is you all put your trust in the wrong people. Because the people in control look like you, you thought you didn't have to keep an eye on them. You forgot what power is all about." There was a bristling feel to the air. But the Black man looked relaxed. "All these lay-offs. You know how much money your union reps are making? Twice what they were ten years ago. I used to be a union man. You don't remember, but I was working out to Homestead when that first big layoff hit twenty years ago. I was 41 years old, with 19 years and 9 months in. Three months to go for retirement. They shut down, and the union told me, sell my time. Only thing you can do, they said. The company will give you $2700 for it. Twenty years ago, that was good money. I had four kids then, I couldn't, like some of them single kids, take a job doing fast food. I had to feed my babies. The union said, sell your time. The mill's never gonna reopen.

"So I took the money. And when the mill started gearing up again, calling back people, it was like I'd never been there. Three months away from a retirement check. Instead, you know what I got now? Three months a year I get a check for $201 from DPA. I get $10 a month food stamps. I mow lawns—when I can borrow a mower. I sell blood down the plasma center with all them dopers. I used to go down to Bio Decision, let them pump me full of drugs—they test pharmaceuticals to see if there are any side effects. But now I can't pass their physical. Wife's gone. Kids are gone. Only time I see my grandbabies, is when the food pantry has cookies they're handing out, so at least I have something to bring 'em."

The man's eyes were tearing up and no one knew what to

say. They all looked away from him, but didn't move. The story gave Timmy a queasy feeling in his stomach. It was just because this guy was Black, he told himself, that he couldn't find any work after he was laid off. Wasn't it? That's not going to happen to me, Timmy thought. He started counting on his fingers how many months he'd been out of work, but the queasiness turned into a dull throb and he stopped counting.

"I see that liar who told me to sell my time driving around in a brand new white Caddy. Nice suit, nice tie. Probably going to the damn opera." He forced out a laugh.

"They got lots of nice new buildings downtown—the Steel building, umm, ummmm, with its glass and all, is one pretty building. And all them other pretty places—the one all mirrors, the PPG. That new hotel, the what-do-you-call it, Vista? Whose vista? A room in there costs more for one night than I make in a month." He looked at the men behind him, than at Timmy. "Who works in them? It's not me. I don't guess them people been calling you boys up neither, have they?"

He sipped from his beer, brushed the foam off his moustache with his fingers. "Yes sir, they got all kinds of opportunity for people who already got opportunities." He nodded to himself, put his hands around his glass. His fingers were long and dry, looked to be dusted with chalk powder. "But I was a union man, through and through. What I am now, I owe it all to the union." He laughed. "And my own stupidity for trusting anyone in power."

No one said anything. The two men returned to the corner. Harry filled the man's mug to the top, then took up the channel changer and clicked through the stations, muttering about all the crap on the tube.

Timmy leaned closer, then slid over one stool. "What was this about, Bio something?"

The man looked closely at Timmy's face. "You got a family?"

"Yeah."

"Man, you don't wanna be doing that, then." The man put his hands flat to the bar, shook his head. "You're in there with all junkies and winos. They shoot you with this stuff—nobody knows what it's gonna do to you. I seen people passing out, going into seizures." He looked at Timmy again. "You need something, go to the Food Pantry."

"I don't know," Timmy said, pushing back on his stool.

"It's not half bad," the man said. He told Timmy about the place, where it was, how it worked. He took a cocktail napkin and, borrowing a pencil from Harry, drew a map. The east side, Timmy saw.

Timmy leaned away from the man. He wanted to ask if white people went, but he didn't want to offend this guy. As if he could read Timmy's mind, the old man told him, "All kinds go there. People just like you. And the ones who run it are nice. They try to make it seem you aren't doing what you are doing." He sipped from his beer, his voice gone soft, tight. "Begging." His head ticked from side to side. "But you go down there today, you'll go home with a bag of groceries."

"Is that why you're here. I mean, is that where you're going?" Timmy asked. "I can, I can...give you a ride."

The man's eyes moved nervously. He hunched closer to the counter. "I appreciate the offer, but I'm applying for them mall jobs."

The booths creaked as the two men shifted in their seats. Timmy looked at the old man. "What jobs?"

The man hooked his thumb at the door. "They're taking applications today. Turning that plant into a shopping mall."

The two men were up again, both yelling at the same time about What's this, What's going on? The old man repeated himself, and the sandy-haired man shook his fleshy face. "What are they telling your people for? We should be getting first crack at it. We live here."

The old man's eyes had narrowed defiantly. "It was in all the papers. Any fool could read about it. Said they're expecting over a thousand people to apply for fifty jobs."

"Fifty." The sandy-haired man scoffed. "After they fill all the quotas, won't be but twenty jobs for regular people."

FAITH IN WHAT?

"Didn't say nothing about no quotas," the old man said, his voice rising. But the two men weren't listening. They were already rushing out the door. The man watched them leave, then turned back to the bar. 'Hell, who's going to hire an old black man in this city anyways?" he said, and he drained off half his beer. "Ain't you going?" he asked Timmy.

Timmy thought about it. Should he go for the job interview, or the bag of food? Sure, he needed work. But he wasn't dressed, and he hadn't had no time to prepare himself, get ready to answer their questions. And a thousand people? What chance did he have? Stand in line all day for what? Most of the interviews he had gone to, he just froze up, started sweating, whenever he was required to speak. The words never came out right—he wasn't a type of person who knew how to talk right. In the end, they always told him, Sorry, you're not exactly the kind of person we're looking for. He was tired of hearing that. What did it mean? And what the hell kind of person was he, anyway? The thought of facing that whole process overwhelmed him. Then, too, if he at least had something to bring home, so he wouldn't have to face Pat empty-handed... "I can definitely get a bag today?" he asked the man. The man nodded. "The hell with it," he told Harry. "Pour me a shot."

Timmy headed east out of the neighborhood, the car bucking, but not stalling. When he reached what he thought of as the 'bad' side of town, he checked to be sure all his doors were locked. The buildings here were full of roaches and rats, the streets littered with garbage and drug dealers. At least, that's what the guys at the plant always used to say. But as he drove along, past streets lined with old victorian three-storied houses which had been turned into apartments, he saw no one but a few children, playing on the sidewalks. There was less trash around than in his own neighborhood.

He looked at the map on the napkin. Following the arrows, he took a right onto a street where boarded-up businesses on one side faced, across a pitted road, four-story apartment buildings made from river rock. Now we get to it, he thought. Have I really sunk this low? A twinge of self-hate ran through him like a sudden headache. He remembered a phrase his friends had used, back in high school, when something unfair had happened to you, you had been denied something you thought you had coming; What am I, a nigger? That didn't seem in the least bit funny, now. Now, he thought he understood a little bit about that man at the bar, what his life must've been like.

The cement church took up an entire block. He parked across the street, in front of a library. He could see through the plate glass window into the library's periodical room. Several old men flipped through magazines while other, younger, men dozed in chairs. Is that what I've got to look forward to? Timmy wondered.

He turned. Before him was a three-way intersection dominated by a fountain. Upon a circular cement base stood a rusted sculpture of six human figures bent backwards, their angular arms linked, their featureless heads tipped up as if to receive the blessing of the water. But there was no water. The basin was empty. The figures seemed bent in pain, or pleas for mercy.

Timmy locked the car and crossed the street to stand in front of the heavy wooden door of the church. Just do it, he told himself. He grabbed the looped iron handle on the door, and yanked it open.

The wood scraped in the frame, gave out a whining complaint, and Timmy tried not to notice those others inside, who turned to stare as he entered. He looked around, not sure where to go. It was a small room cluttered with five long folding tables of the type used for church picnics. There were no windows and the fluorescent lights glared off the beige walls, the black-grimed cement floor. Less than a dozen people, most of them women, all but two black, sat in attitudes of resignation. Several smoked, using tuna fish cans, stripped of their labels, for ashtrays. One woman held a small baby wrapped in a cloth blanket in her lap. An old man wearing a brown, wide-brimmed hat, seeing Timmy's confusion, raised a sticklike arm and motioned towards a walkway at the far side of the room. Timmy gave a quick nod of thanks without letting the man catch his eye. He ducked his head, telling himself, I'm not like these people. This is just a one-time thing for me. These people are losers. I don't belong here.

The walkway was blocked by a desk covered with green cardboard filing boxes brimming with white cards. He'd been expecting to see a priest, or at least a nun—the church ran this didn't they?—and was startled to be confronted by a beautiful black woman wearing an angora sweater, smiling up at him.

"Hi. I.D.?" she said. She had skin the color of rawhide, large brown eyes highlighted by thick bands of purple glitter eyeshadow. Her wide, curling smile revealed teeth that were slightly bucked and so white he thought they must be painted.

When he hesitated, she asked if he'd been there before. Timmy was able to manage a brief shake of his head. He tried not to look at her, but it was worse turning to face the others in the room. "First time," he managed, looking down at her hands, long and smooth, ending in nails which were painted to match her eyeshadow.

"Everybody has a first time," she said, her voice low and husky. "I need something with your name and address on it." For a second, Timmy thought she was coming on to him. Then she pulled out a blank file. He blushed.

He seemed to be fumbling everything as he searched his wallet for his license. He pulled out his cards and kept sorting through them, but couldn't find it. His face felt hot, and he could make out distinct rivulets of sweat seeping from his armpits down his sides. She reached forward, touched his hand, stopping him, then pulled his license out.

"This'll be fine," she told him. As she bent, he looked at the way her gold-streaked straight hair hung in bangs at her forehead, covered her ears. "How many in your household?" she asked.

He hesitated. Sweat began to form on his brow. "Ahm, myself, my..wife, my daughter Ellen..."

37

"How old is she?"

"Six."

"That's a great age." She gave him that wide smile. "Mine, too. What school does your daughter go to? She's in first grade, right?"

He looked at this woman, her lively eyes, her smile, and his mind went blank. He swore he could feel everyone in the room watching him, listening. He thought hard, but he couldn't remember the name of Ellen's school. His hands closed at his sides and he squeezed them.

"I'm sorry," the woman said, "you're probably in a hurry. Let me just finish this for you. Let's see, any other children?"

The sweat was so heavy on his forehead it began to run into his eyes, stinging them so that he had to wipe it away. If he told her about Katie, she'd ask how old. She might ask what grade Katie was in, what school she went to. He'd have to tell the whole story, right here, in front of everyone. "No," Timmy said. "Just, I just...the one."

She set the card on top of a pile to her right and told him to have a seat until his name was called.

He moved to the far corner, hating himself for denying his own child. He felt his betrayal of her as a sharp yoke, bending down his neck. Katie, I'm sorry, he told her in his mind. You know you were always my favorite. Were? he thought, and he told himself, she's not dead. Truth is, he thought, since he'd lost his job, for all the thinking he'd done about any of them—Katie, Pat, or Ellen—they might as well have been dead. He'd been so consumed with his own problems, he hardly had time to even remember he was part of a family.

He took a seat at the rear of the table furthest from the desk. The chair backed onto a door with a small, wooden sign above it. Gouged into the wood by a wood-carving iron—he could tell by the bumpy charred ditches of the letters—were the words, Good Samaritan Shelter.

Timmy rose and looked through the small square pane in the door. He noted about ten sets of bunkbeds, separated by individual stand-up lockers. At the far end of the alcove, a stained-glass window depicting Christ the shepherd, staff in hand, lamb nestled at his feet, glowed vividly. He turned from it.

I don't belong here, Timmy told himself as he settled into a folding metal chair. I should just get up and leave. He looked around. The woman with the baby was sharing a low, laughing conversation with the old man who'd directed Timmy to the desk. The man waved his hat at the baby, who gurgled happily. Everyone else in the room was silent, their looks indrawn, as if they were trying to pretend they weren't there, doing what they were doing. Timmy looked at the baby again.

When his own children were that small, he was terrified that something bad might happen to them—an accident, a fall. Although he never really believed anything would happen, not to his kids. And then what happened to Katie was worse than anything he could ever imagine. And now, here he was, here. Imagine if he'd had to bring them here with him, if his life, when they were babies, was so bad off this was a regular part of their routine. In its own way, wouldn't that be just as great a tragedy? He thought of the stained glass window. Jesus was supposed to take care of kids, Timmy thought. What happened? Even after Katie got sick, Timmy spoke in his mind, I still believed in You. I begged You for five years to make her better. And You didn't do nothing to help her. Now You let them humiliate me at the Unemployment—for what? What did I say that was so bad? Even if I did say something, why are you making my family suffer? You let them take my check away. You got me here begging for scraps. You got this other woman and her baby here. What's wrong with You?

He rose from his seat. I don't need this, he told himself. I'm not going to take this. This isn't me, this isn't who I've become. I'm not like these people. I'm not this desperate. I can get by. From the room behind the desk, a man came forward clutching a brown bag full of groceries in one arm, a plastic bag stuffed with bread in the other.

Timmy sat back down. He was like these people. He did

need the food. Even more, Timmy needed to be able to bring something home. Not just so Pat wouldn't yell at him—he didn't know what to tell her about his check. But he needed to feel that in some way he was providing for his family. Christmas was coming—forget Thanksgiving, he'd already written that off —and he was afraid it was going to be just like last year, when they had to wait until Christmas Eve, and the trees were free, before they could get one. Then they'd had so few presents, even spreading them out didn't help. It took two minutes to open them all and then Timmy, Pat, and Ellen looked at each other like, What were they going to do with the rest of the day? And Ellen trying to pretend she wasn't disappointed.

This whole past year had been like that, things had been so tight. Timmy felt he'd become an embarrassment to his kids. He'd taken to scavenging; hunting for marked-down, bruised food in the supermarkets; sorting through someone else's throwaways down the Goodwill to find school outfits for Ellen, clothes for Katie. He even spent one day picking up cans along the highway, for the nickel deposits, until a car full of high school kids raced by, beeping the horn, everyone laughing at him.

Each day, Timmy felt more worthless. He was running out of options, finding it harder to make it look like he had some purpose in his life, like he had something to do with his time. He hated himself for wanting this bag of groceries, for needing it. But he knew he did. He needed something. Just so he could look Pat in the eyes and show her he still had some value left.

Chapter 5

BY THE TIME the afternoon session was over, Timmy was home from unemployment. He came down to help me carry Katie up the stairs. I could smell the beer on him. On the one hand, What's the big deal? I thought. Stopping for a beer or two. On the other hand—here we were scraping pennies. I didn't feel like I had the energy to get into it, so I said nothing.

He gripped Katie under her arms, and I held her feet. He went first, walking backwards up the stairs. Sometimes I went too fast for him, sometimes too slow. We kept pushing Katie back and forth as if she were an accordian. There was something strange about his mood. It was almost like he was happy. That made me mad. It's easy to smile if you haven't spent your whole afternoon in the cellar, I thought to myself. If you've got a buzz on from planting your ass in some barroom. Maybe I'd go out and get loaded myself, I thought. Tonight, when it was Timmy's turn to do the patterning. See how he liked it.

The staircase emptied into the dining area, a small space open to the living room and separated from the kitchen by a waist-high divider. The first time Timmy was laid off, we'd panicked and sold off most of our good furniture, including the mahogany dining set my mother had given us for a wedding present. What was I supposed to do? I had to take care of my family. Still, I felt bad. It was really the only thing I had from my mother. My girlfriends, they had stuff like necklaces or rings their mothers had given them. But my mother wasn't like that. I mean, she was the type, when it was raining out or something, she'd put on my dad's rubber boots to pick us up at school.

Anyways, we got $125 for the table and six chairs, and bought a $50 set from Goodwill; a fiberboard table with a fake formica top, and four chairs shaped like flattened highway cones. They were covered with gold vinyl that had these huge, ugly orange flowers embedded in it. I remember Timmy saying, after I'd decided that was the best we could afford, "I thought you always said we needed, or were gonna need, six chairs."

He'd been looking through an assortment of little boys' baseball bats stuck in a wastebasket, and he picked one out and stood up, running his hand slowly over the scarred, grained wood. He gave me that smile of his—that sort of hopeful, shy, conspiratorial smile he showed those times when we had an afternoon off together with nobody around.

"That was before Katie," I told him. He never brought it up again.

While he settled her now in the wheelchair in front of the TV, I went into the kitchen to try to figure out something for supper. On the counter beside the sink I found a paper bag full of groceries, and a plastic bag packed with bread.

"What's this?" I called.

He flicked on Sesame Street then came and leaned on the divider. He grinned, but it was an uneasy grin, and he turned away.

I unloaded spaghetti, spaghetti sauce, peanut butter, canned beans—all generic. I pulled out a large silver can with a black sketch of a pig on the front and the letters USDA over the word PORK. The flour and the honey were government surplus, too. "Oh no, Timmy, you didn't," I said. "Handouts?" I felt a sudden urgency to hide this from Ellen and I looked over to be sure she wasn't watching. She glanced at me, her face confused, uncertain.

At the bottom of the bag were a box labelled Farfel, and a can with no label. "What is this crap?" I held them up to Timmy.

His eyes seemed to grow small and dark and sink deeper into his face. As he curled his lower lip under his top teeth, his moustache hid his mouth. "You're welcome," he said, heading back for the living room.

"Don't turn your back on me," I said.

He stopped on the threshhold of the living room and turned around. "That's funny, coming from you."

I could see Ellen watching. Beyond her, Katie slouched sideways in her chair, sucking on her hand, seeing nothing.

"What do you mean by that?" I asked, though I had an idea. I knew I'd been difficult to live with lately. Everything seemed to be piling up on me. I was just about ready to apologize, when I realized there had only been the one bag of groceries on the counter. "Didn't you go shopping?" I asked. "If you drank up your check..."

His head tipped slowly upwards until he was staring at the ceiling . "I didn 't get a check " he said softly.

"You what?" I nearly yelled, I was so surprised.

"It wasn't my fault. There was some...mix-up."

"Mix-up?" I said. I couldn't stop shaking my head. "Oh, that's just great." I'd had every penny spent and I didn't even want to think about the letters I'd have to write, the phone calls —talking to people who made you feel this big whenever you couldn't pay them. College kids who just because they had a degree could get work sitting on their asses harassing people like us for money.

"Well, *you* can tell Mary Catherine tonight that we can't pay her for the construction paper I asked her to pick up. "

"I'm not going to tonight's crew," he said.

"What's that?" I took a step towards him.

He turned his head from side to side, shuffled a bit. "This is the first Monday night the Steelers been on in years—don't you remember? I told you. All the guys from the plant are going to Gerry's."

I paused for a few seconds—I didn't remember, but he might have told me—then started putting things away, slamming the cupboards. "You never even liked the Steelers all that much."

"It ain't the game, Pat. It's a chance to get together with the guys." He came around and put his hands to the top of one of the chairs. "I told you a month ago."

I felt like I was being accused of something and all I could think to do was strike back. "How do you expect me to remember everything you mumble? I bust my ass in here every day, trying to keep the program together, then I haul my ass around the city selling that Amway crap so's we can have some money coming in, and all you give a shit about is football." He didn't say anything, so I told him, "I wish I had time to sit around and bullshit with my friends."

"You wish you had friends," he said, his voice so cold it chilled, going through. I gripped the counter by the sink and looked out into our back yard, the grass gone brown, the small maple gray and bare of leaves. "I'm sorry, Pat, I shouldn't have said that."

He came over and put his hands on my shoulders. I ducked away from him and pulled a spaghetti pan out from underneath the stove. "It's just one night," he said. "Can't we skip the program for one night?"

"It's one night for you." I whirled and pointed my finger in his face. "But it's her life." I pointed at Katie. "How many times a week do we have to skip because we don't have a crew? Tonight we got people willing to come over and you want to blow it off."

"I can't hear the show," Ellen said. She'd slipped off the couch and was standing, leaning against the arm, her hands over her ears.

"I'll do the first hour," Timmy said, looking at her. "You can take over after that. Some day you want a break, I'll cover for you. That fair?"

"Do what you want," I said. I blasted water from the faucet to fill the pan and banged it onto the stove.

"Why are you fighting me? We're on the same side. I'm not the enemy." He came closer, his hands reaching, pulling on mine, trying to turn me to face him. "Hey," he said. "Hey. C'mon now. We got to help each other. Give me a little hug."

I yanked my hands away and washed them in the sink. "No."

"Why not?"

"Because I am so pissed off at you it scares me. Nothing in my life turned out the way I wanted it to."

He lost it then. "I suppose that's my fault, too? I did this on purpose." His sweeping arm took in everything. "You think this is the way *I* wanted it?" He pounded his fist on the counter.

From the living room came one, sharp sob. I looked over in time to see Ellen's legs—her ankle socks and shiny black shoes —as she ran up the stairs. "Ellen, honey," I shouted, hurrying over. I looked up at an empty stairway and heard her door slam. It would be useless, I knew, to try to get into her room.

I felt Timmy right behind me. I was afraid he was going to hold me. Turning, I shook my hands once, hard, at the floor. "See what you've done?" I said, and I pushed past him into the kitchen.

Ellen was still upstairs when the crew arrived. She'd refused to join us for supper, and I'd left a plate of spaghetti on the rug outside her room. It was still there two hours later, when I tapped on her door.

"Hey, you cooling this down to make spaghetti pudding?" I said. Silence. "You want me to heat it up for you?" Nothing. I tapped again. "Daddy's leaving. I'll be in the cellar if you need anything." I thought I heard her make one of those smacking sounds of derision. But I wasn't sure.

In the cellar, Timmy tried to give me a kiss before he left. I turned quickly, pretending I hadn't noticed him coming towards me with his arms open, and busied myself picking lint off the floor. The volunteers had noticed, though. I could tell by how silent they were when I stood up.

"Well," I said, pausing to listen to Timmy cross the room above us, then bang shut the door. I looked down at Katie. "This is going to sound crazy," I told the crew. "But I don't think she's as damaged as everyone thinks." I put my face close to Katie's and whispered, "I don't know what's in your head, but I wish it'd get out." Raising my head up, I said, "Know what I think?"

"Uh-oh, we're in trouble. Pat's thinking again," Patrice said. Everyone laughed. Patrice, who's in her fifties, was wearing a red-and-white striped man's pullover jersey, though she's never been married. Her hair is permed tight to her head, and dyed a dark chestnut. The way her cheeks and throat hang loose, it looks like they're melting. And her teeth are so widely spaced and yellowed that she looks frightening when she smiles. Ellen won't come down when she's here, which is too bad, because Patrice is a stitch and has a heart the size of this room.

"I'm serious now," I said. "I think one day she's just going to get up. Just like that, and it'll be all over. She'll be back again. Ain't that right Katie?" I leaned my face down and rubbed her nose with mine. Her eyes shifted from side to side, as if I wasn't even there.

No one said anything. They stood quietly, and I could tell they were embarrassed. I looked around at the five women. They were all from the Senior Citizens' Center; Timmy called this group my 'Blue-Haired Ladies Crew,' though only two of them have blue hair.

"Well, let's get this show on the road," I said.

There's a whole program of exercises we have to run through. I'd first read about it in a READER'S DIGEST. Katie had been home for two months and I was getting desperate. The doctors at the hospital in Pittsburgh told me there was nothing to do for her. I felt like I was sitting home, just watching her rot. Then I read about this doctor from Philadelphia who had developed this experimental program for brain-damaged kids. Patterning, it's called. He designed this series of exercises that were supposed to make your child's nerves send signals to the cells in their brain that were still good, the cells that hadn't been damaged. Like, if the right side of your head was gone, the nerves would send signals to your left side. Over time, a pattern would develop in these good cells, and they'd take over the functions that used to be performed by the cells that had been destroyed. It was a long shot, but hey, it was the only shot we had. We packed up the car and drove out there and, with the money we'd saved from Timmy's job, we could just afford to get in on it.

They gave us this whole list of things to do with Katie at home. It was a long process, and you had to go through a series of exercises in an exact order. First, you exercised each limb individually, sort of loosening them; right arm, left arm, right leg, left leg. Then—and this is why I needed so many volunteers, this and the fact that the whole program is supposed to be done twice a day, seven days a week—everyone would take a limb, and one person the head, and you'd have to co-ordinate the movements to make the child's body move. After that, you put her through the routine on the floor. It was like your kid had to go back to the beginning, back past the point where a baby learns how to crawl. She had to start all over from square one, learn how to be human again.

I took Katie's right leg, pulled her knee towards me, and slid the bottom of her foot along the inside of her left leg until her heel touched her bum. Then I raised her knee so that it was bent, pointing at the ceiling, and I slid her leg down flat again. Patrice, who's been with me since the beginning, repeated the movement with Katie's left leg. We alternated, fifty repetitions each.

It took four of us to flip Katie over onto her stomach. She was solid and heavy, since she couldn't move herself. Joyce and Mary Catherine, the two blue-hairs, took up positions on opposite sides of the table to work on Katie's arms. They placed her palms flat, pointing forward, then lowered her elbows down to the vinyl surface of the table, so that Katie's arms made triangles pointing at each woman.

I moved to the head of the table and slid on the cloth gloves so I could hold Katie's face up. If you didn't hold it, her cheeks would brush against the vinyl and break out in a rash. The ladies took turns holding down Katie's hands and pushing her elbows up to point at the ceiling. Katie ground her teeth loudly and started to moan.

"Stop it," I told her. "You behave now." She jerked her head and I had to wrestle with it to keep it still. "Don't be a brat. Stop being so stubborn. This is for your own good."

Katie ceased fighting and Patrice said from the foot of the table, "See, she understands you. C'mon, Katie. C'mon, Champ."

Mary Catherine, who has a granddaughter Katie's age, jiggled Katie's right arm. It had stiffened and Mary Catherine couldn't move it. Katie raised her head and let loose a throaty gasp of pain that didn't sound human. It made me shiver. Though I heard that sound often, I never got used to it.

"It's okay honey, it's all right now," Mary Catherine said in that soft way she has of talking, like she's a living Hallmark card. She's a big woman, with smooth, white white skin, and though her voice is quiet, you can't help listening. She began to hum "Mary Has a Little Lamb."

Katie howled.

"That's a good sign. She's getting mad. We'll get some work out of her today," Patrice said.

I knew Patrice was right. Katie always did better when she was crying and in pain. But it made me feel two feet tall, knowing the only time she made progress was when she was in agony.

Katie wailed the whole time they were moving her arms.

We lifted her, next, onto the floor, her stomach to the brown, acrylic rug Timmy had installed himself. It was bunched in parts, and loose, and was either short of the walls or ran up them. He felt terrible about it but I told him, hey, it served its function. Everyone got down slowly to their knees, took an arm or a leg. I held her head.

This was the full patterning. We had to make her crawl. Her right arm and left leg would be pushed forward, her head turned to the left, then we'd reverse and bring her left arm and right leg forward, her head turned to the right. Katie was supposed to pull with her own arms, push off with her feet. But usually we ended up sliding her along the floor.

"C'mon, don't be lazy," Patrice said, jiggling Katie's right leg. "Let's go."

FAITH IN WHAT?

Katie lay motionless.

"All right, let's push her though," I told them.

The minute we started to move her limbs, slide her along the rug, Katie began screaming. She howled in a steady, high-pitched note, as if there were a strange animal inside her, trying to get out. It was a different sound than she'd made before, and it made me nervous—what with the startle-reactions she'd been having lately. But I told the ladies, "Push her through."

She fought us, cramping her limbs, pulling them into herself, raising her head to cry louder. My head started pounding so bad I wanted to just cut into it to relieve the pressure. "C'mon," I said, "Don't be stubborn." But Katie wouldn't stop screaming, fighting us. It got so bad I wanted to slap her, shake her, anything, just to get her to cooperate. "You're killing me," I said, as we reached the end of the room. We had to stand to lift her to turn her around.

When we set her down and got in position again, her bowels released with a muffled sound of puttering air. Everyone let go and inched away from her. "Good," I said. "That's just great. Are you happy now?" I angled her face towards mine. She was smiling, though not at me.

We lifted her onto the table. I asked the ladies to go to the corner for a second, out of respect for Katie. I undid her Huggies. The sight of her mess, the fact that she couldn't even use a toilet, seemed worse than the brain damage. "What am I gonna do with you?" I whispered. Eleven years old, I thought, running my hand down her long, tight legs. "Thank God you're thin like Timmy."

"You can say that again," Patrice called over. "One Pillsbury Dough Boy per family is enough."

"No one asked you," I said, pretending to be mad so the ladies could all have a laugh. I looked at Katie and tried to think about what her life would be like, if this hadn't happened. With her build and all, and Timmy crazy about sports, and things different for girls now, more open than when I went to school, Katie would probably be into gymnastics, or basketball. We'd be going to the school on weekends, our whole family, sitting on those long bleachers in the gym to root Katie on. Instead...

49

I cleaned her carefully with the paper towels. A small, downy flame of pubic hair was just sprouting between her legs. Jesus, I thought, what do you want from me? Let her get up. Let her say Mumma. Let her do anything. My baby. My girl.

Chapter 6

THE CAR WAS BUCKING as he drove north on Negley Avenue. At the intersection with Stanton Avenue, Timmy floored the gas and spun the steering wheel hard to his left. The car slid across the intersection, fishtailed. The people on the corner to his right, standing at the bus stop in front of a huge, black stone church, turned frightfully towards him. Timmy felt the need to explain himself, although he knew that was a stupid idea. What was he going to do? Park the car, leave it running, and hop out to tell them his problems? Nobody wanted to hear his problems. Not even Pat. If it didn't have to do with Katie, she didn't care. She didn't see all the garbage piling up so high around them they were all beginning to suffocate.

Yeah, well, maybe you're having trouble seeing, too, Timmy told himself. I mean, look at Katie, look at Pat, look at Ellen for Chrissakes. He shook his head as he continued west on Stanton. Until he got his own ass straightened out, he didn't want to even think about anybody else.

He drove past three-story brick buildings with turret rooms and stained glass windows over the front doors. Families had once lived in these places, and he wondered, Who the hell ever had the money for that? Now, though, they'd all been turned into rental units and were looking pretty rundown. The bricks needed to be repointed. The trim painted. He could imagine the type of people who lived in them now.

On a lighted porch to his right, he saw a group of Spanish-looking men playing guitars and beating on long drums with their hands. He felt a swift surge of anger. Shouldn't those people be inside, waiting for the Steelers' kickoff? Showing their support for the team? For Pittsburgh? They probably don't even speak English. He wondered if they worked, or were on welfare. He didn't know which would be worse. Then he told himself, C'mon Timmy, what's wrong with you? "It's so hard," he argued aloud in the car. "When things ain't working out in your life, how can you care what's happening in somebody else's?"

He turned right onto the next street and the car stalled. It drifted down the slight decline of the road and he tried to jump start it. No luck. He let it coast a block, then hauled on the steering wheel with both hands. He was able to veer the car to the curb beside a fire hydrant. Screw it, he thought, cutting his lights and locking the doors. No one would be out ticketing when the Steelers were on.

Gerry's building stood out like a tumor. It was a six-unit box with weathered-brown stucco walls. What made it even more obvious tonight, was the way Gerry had decorated the place. A yellow banner with STEELERS PARTY lettered in black hung between the two front windows of his second floor apartment. The windows themselves were criss-crossed with black and yellow streamers. Strings of small, white bulbs blinked along the window frames.

Timmy felt a flutter of excitement. The idea of crowding into a room full of people, everyone joking and drinking, slapping five, pounding each other on their backs—it would be just like the old times at Harry's, where, on pay days, the shots and beers would be lined up sometimes five and six deep. By the time the guys made it home, suppers and children would've been long since put away, and their wives would be alternately disgusted, accepting, and, if their husbands didn't pass out, willing to put up with that drunken rutting the men sought as if it were the culminating ritual of pay day.

Timmy hit Gerry's buzzer impatiently.

Yeah?" came Gerry's growlly voice out of a staticy silence.

"The Steel Curtain's back," Timmy said, feeling a rush of enthusiasm. He remembered being a kid in the 1970s, when everyone in the city was caught up in the excitement of the Steelers going again and again to the Superbowl. Man, if he could get that feeling back. The door buzzed open and he bounded inside.

Black and gold streamers were twined up the railing of the stairs. On Gerry's door was an old poster of Mean Joe Greene, arms raised like an enraged animal as he bore down on a quarterback. Before Timmy could pound on the wood, Gerry swung the door open.

"Steelers, Steelers," he chanted. He wore a Steelers sweatshirt and cap and waved a white towel like a lasso over his head. With his long, unshaped hair and beard, he looked, Timmy thought, like one of those guitar players in a Southern band.

"All the way," Timmy said, pumping one fist. "No one's spitting in our face this year."

"Hoo hoo hoo," Gerry grunted. He put a hand to Timmy's neck and jerked his face forward so their heads butted.

The black and gold streamers were everywhere—taped to the walls, draped from the ceiling. Black and gold balloons clustered in the corners of the spacious front room. On every open space—end table, lamp stand, all across the eating counter by the kitchen—family-sized bags of barbecue chips, nachos, and popcorn stood open in invitation. At the base of the counter where it met the wall were stacked several boxes of pizza, the smell of melted cheese and pepperoni filling the air. The silver head of a keg loomed up from its perch atop a chair beside the refrigerator.

The TV was on, but the sound turned down in favor of the radio broadcast. Timmy listened to the nasal, whining tone of Myron Pope, a Pittsburgh sportscasting institution. With his popping eyes, narrow pointed face, and high-pitched, smarmy voice, Myron seemed more suited for selling cheap wine than broadcasting a football game. And even Timmy got tired sometimes of his excited complaints about the often-imaginary injustices inflicted on the Steelers by the referees. The man was an embarassment. Still, he was Pittsburgh's own.

"Myron's ripe tonight," Gerry said as the announcer grunted, "Hoo haw, umm." Gerry sat on the couch opposite the TV and motioned to Timmy to pick a seat. Timmy sat on the other end of the couch. He grinned at Gerry. Gerry grinned back.

"All right," Gerry said.

"All right," said Timmy. He looked around at the streamers, the balloons, the food, the TV. It took him a few seconds to realize there was no one else there.

By the end of the first quarter, Chuck Daniels had arrived. A tall, sloe-eyed man, Chuck always looked like he was a day behind in his shaving. His expression was slow to change, his responses often distracted, like someone who is constantly stoned. Yet he moved with a surprising grace. Chuck, like Gerry, had worked in a different section of the plant, so Timmy knew them only because they went to Harry's after work.

Chuck settled in a recliner separated from Timmy by a lamp stand. The space between Timmy and Gerry, to Timmy's right, seemed greater than the span of one couch cushion. In the bar, it had been easy to talk, swap good-natured gripes about wives, sports, work. Here, they all seemed uncomfortable, as if unsure what was allowed. Occasionally one of them might shout their appreciation when a Steeler hit someone from the other team hard enough to cause an injury. But mostly they sat silent, not even rising for food or drink.

When the game broke for halftime, Timmy realized he didn't know the score. He didn't even know who was winning. What had he been thinking about? He had no idea. This is ridiculous anyways, he thought, sitting around, watching people younger than him, making more money than he'd make in ten years, smack into each other, trying to put each other out of work. He should've just stayed home. He could've spent some time with Ellen, or helped put Katie to bed, or tried to talk to Pat. Done something that would bring him together with his family, and *still* have watched the game. Even as he thought that, he knew those things wouldn't have happened, not in the way he imagined them. Home would've been a place of disappointment, of silence and accusations. He did need to get away from that. But he felt cheated, because this here wasn't doing nothing for him, either. He didn't know what he wanted it to do, but it was supposed to be some help.

He went to the kitchen to draw a plastic cup full of beer, his second, and wondered about all the people at the Stadium watching this game, getting drunk and rowdy. Guys who would go home to wives and kids who were happy to see them. Not like his family, where, Timmy felt, everyone was watching him, waiting for him to make a wrong move. Of course those guys at the Stadium, if they could afford tickets they obviously had jobs to go to tomorrow; places where there were other guys to rehash the game with, so it became something that mattered.

Back in the living room, Gerry had changed the channel. The news was on. "I need to see something. You mind?"

"No," Chuck said. Timmy nodded his approval, told Gerry, "I got to get going soon anyways."

"For what?" Gerry asked.

Timmy turned from Gerry to the screen. The news anchors were an older-man, younger-woman tag team, Will Breece and Sandy Cooper. Will, a dull-looking sixtiesh man with glasses and wispy hair blown wild in front, had recently been criticised for suggesting the city could solve its pigeon problem by killing the birds and sending them to the starving people in Africa. Black leaders were outraged. All the old-time Pittsburghers had rallied to Will's defense.

Sandy was a thirtyish woman of such nondescript, dark-haired attractiveness, that once the TV was off you forgot what she looked like. She had recently returned from China, where she'd done a series of reports focusing on the lack of amenities like chipped ham, the filthiness of Chinese bathrooms, and how the chefs weren't able to cook Chinese food the way Pittsburghers liked it. Rumors about her changed with the seasons; she was so brilliant she could've been a rocket scientist; she was so dumb she couldn't add two plus two. The only rumor that never changed was the one that said she was making a million bucks a year. Every time Timmy thought about that, his jaw tightened, his teeth ground together. She didn't even have a family to support. What the hell did she need the money for? And to be paid that kind of money to read words off a cue card—no wonder the country was going to hell.

Will Breece read the lead story, about a man who'd come to be known as The Hardhat Bandit. He wore a hardhat and goggles and a long blue bandana which covered his nose and mouth and was tucked into the zipped-up collar of his white Barracuda jacket. He robbed small branches of major banks. He'd hit one today, his third this week.

"Police theorize," Will said, "that he may be a laid-off blue collar worker who mistakenly is blaming the banks for his plight."

"Mistaken my ass," Gerry said, clicking the TV off. "They're all in it together, the banks and the bosses and the businessmen."

"The Killer B's," Chuck said. In took a few seconds for Gerry and Timmy to catch on.

"See what they're doing to the plant?" Gerry asked.

Timmy remembered what the Black man had told him earlier, at Harry's. "Making a mall?"

"Yeah, " Gerry said. "You can bet your ass they had this planned when they shut it down." His mouth opened in a mean smile, showing teeth that were small and yellowed. "First the mall, next you're gonna see yuppies buying up all the housing dirt cheap from people who can't pay their mortgages anymore. Then places like Harry's will close, and you'll see all these new joints opening with plants and imported beers. You won't be able to buy a kielbasa sandwich in this city anymore, it'll be all this quiche and vegetables and shit you can't pronounce the names of. Coffee in a cup the size of your thumb with fucking *whipped cream* on top. All part of the Mayor's Pittsburgh Renaissance. Hey, renaissance this." He grabbed his crotch.

Chuck folded his hands behind his head. "Yeah, but at least they're gonna give the laid-off workers first crack at the 'employment opportunities'," he said, turning the phrase to make a joke of it.

Gerry gave him a scornful look. "What opportunities? Selling records to high school kids? Scooping cones of ice cream? Who's gonna hire someone looks like me to sell suit coats? And even if you could get put on the payroll, you know what it's gonna be? Permanent part-time, minimum wage, no benefits. Just wait and see. You know that McDonald's down the center, the new one? A hundred and ten employees, all part-time. Can you live on that crap? Lose all your medical benefits and shit for eighty bucks a week? Hell, I don't even have a family and I can't afford to take it. They're just jerking us around, trying to bust our balls. Trying to push our asses out of this city now that they don't have no need for us anymore."

"I don't know if I can listen to this," Timmy said. He shook his head, his eyes narrowing as he focused his gaze on the scuffed toes of his workboots.

"Well, you better listen, because they're taking our fucking life away. They're trying to make us extinct."

"Jim said something like that, too," Timmy nodded.

"Hey, everyone knows it. It's no big secret—except to the smiling clowns like that." Gerry motioned at the TV.

Chuck leaned forward, his long arms curving out as he gripped his hands over one knee. "My poetry teacher says we're on the verge of a worker's revolution."

Oh man, Timmy thought. Poetry again? What is this stuff, contagious? He looked at Gerry, who was glancing at Chuck suspiciously. "Poetry teacher?" Gerry asked.

"Yeah."

"You mean like, there was a young lady from France, who was always dropping her pants?"

"No not like that. It doesn't even rhyme. It's personal stuff, about your feelings."

Gerry slowly stroked his beard. He shot Timmy a look, gave out a half-laugh of discomfort. "Feelings, huh?" Gerry asked.

Chuck pushed back in his seat so the recliner unfolded. He pulled himself up and looked around the lampstand at Gerry. "Well, feelings and politics. Theodore says everything is politics."

"Theodore?" Gerry tensed visibly. "Not Ted, not Teddy. Theodore?"

Timmy edged closer to the middle of the couch. And he'd always thought Chuck was an okay guy. Now he made a mental note never to be caught in a locker room with him.

"Yeah, Theodore. He's the teacher. He says that by having us write poetry, we can learn how to think critically, and then we won't do stupid things like vote for Reagan."

"Oh, so he's a liberal faggot." Gerry said. "What's he from, San Francisco? Better be careful, Chuck. You know what they say, once you switch, you'll never go back."

"No, he ain't like that. He's from Pittsburgh."

"With a name like Theodore?"

"Maybe it's his teaching name. You know, like actors got stage names?"

Timmy and Gerry mulled that over for a few moments. Chuck leaned forward, making a chopping motion with his hand. "The point is this...what he says makes sense, you know? It makes you look at things differently. Like he talks about how the words people use oppress us, and..."

"What's this got to do with job training?" Timmy asked.

"Don't you see?" Gerry opened his hands and eyes wide. "You go to a construction sight, and when they ask if you can drive heavy machinery, you tell them, No, but I can write a poem about it. Who's not gonna hire you?"

Chuck waved his hand, exasperated. "You guys" he said. He left to draw himself another beer.

When he returned he shrugged his shoulders, his shoulder bones coming up to flank his head like the tines on a fork lift. He told them, "I know it sounds stupid, trying to explain it, but it's not that bad. You just sit around in a room, he reads some of his poems, he has us write some poems about our lives, then he tells us what's wrong with our poems and he takes our, our stories, our material he calls it, and writes his own poems from that. He does that because we're not good enough yet and he thinks it's important to get our—he calls it voice—out. The best way to do that is for him to use our stuff, our material, for his work. It's just an experimental part of this job training program."

Gerry pushed forward, seemed on the verge of rising. "Why don't they experiment with giving us work?" He downed his beer, wiped the foam off his lips. Rage seemed to be taking him over like something alive within him, pushing its way out through his skin. "This is a fuckin' college student?"

"Professor," Chuck said, pulling back a little in his seat.

"Where does that asshole get off?" Gerry was inflamed now, his face flushed, his small dark eyes seeming to come forward as he squinted. "Says he has to teach us how to think? Has he ever been on the dole? Has he ever filled out a fuckin' unemployment or DPA form? Does he know who the ward bosses are, or how you pay them off, or how much it costs for a union card? Did this asshole tell you how much he's making to be in this job training program? How much he's making to fuckin' steal your life and sell it for his own?"

Chuck went tight-lipped in his chair.

"Hey, hey now guys, c'mon," Timmy said. "I mean, what are we talking about here? It's nothing, it's just stupid poems."

"It's oppression." Gerry stood up, hiked his dungarees over his round belly. He shook his finger in Chuck's face. "He's using you like everybody else. He takes your money—takes your, what did you call it, material?" He sat back down, pulled his fingers rapidly through his beard. Nobody helps you. That's what I found out. Nobody gives you a fuckin' thing." He crushed his plastic cup and looked at the flattened disc, then up at Timmy. "The only way you're gonna get something is to take it. That hardhat bandit..." He pointed at the dead TV screen. Timmy

59

turned. He could see the three of them reflected on the green-gray screen, all of them distorted, bowed like the images in a fun house mirror. Gerry leaned back in the couch, his head tipped towards the ceiling. "That guy knows the score. This ain't Pittsburgh without people like us. If we can't get help when we're down..." The brow over his right eye rose slowly. "What's wrong with taking what you need?"

Chapter 7

PATRICE AND MARY CATHERINE helped me carry Katie to her
room. I went up the stairs first, holding onto her arms. Each of
them held one of her legs. It was funny because they kept banging
into each other all the way up. "Hip check," Patrice would say as
she knocked Mary Catherine into the wall. Or, "Bump and run."
At the top, when we set Katie down to catch our breaths, wipe the
sweat off our foreheads, Patrice said, "I feel like that black guy
in "Showboat"." She started singing, "Lift that barge, you gotta
tote that bale." We all laughed, then Patrice bent to Katie and
kissed her forehead. "Just kidding, Champ."

They helped me get her pajamas on and put her to bed.
Timmy had rigged up a railing made from nailed-together two-
by-fours, with a piece of plywood hammered on the bottom that
slid between the mattress and the box spring, to keep the railing
from moving. For extra precautions, I also tied pieces of twine
around the ends of the railing and her bedposts. The way it looked
once it was in place, it reminded me of a cattle crate. It made me
sick at heart. But what could I do?

I told the girls to let themselves out, and I stayed there,
looking at Katie. There hasn't been a day done by I haven't gone
over everything in my head—her going outside, the stay at the
rehab, her doctors. It's like I can't get out of the past. I know it's
crazy, but I keep thinking I can still change things, say or do
something different, make them keep Katie at the rehab until they

find a cure. I think this even though I don't trust doctors or hospitals. I don't believe in them anymore.

I checked on Ellen. She was snoring, her mouth open, and I kissed her forehead, pulled the blanket to her chin. I made sure her books and homework were piled on her bureau, ready for tomorrow. Before closing her door, I stood by her pillow. "Honey, I'm sorry. This is tough on you. you must feel like you don't even have a Mummy and Daddy sometimes." I felt bad, thinking about how she'd spent the whole night by herself. Got ready for bed alone. Crawled under the covers with no one to say good night to. I wanted to hate Timmy for not being here but, Jesus, how much can he take, too? I didn't know how people did it—dealt with something really bad happening and kept your family together.

I went to the bathroom to pee. Sitting on the toilet, I found myself thinking to God, We've had more than our share of bad luck. And I don't want to hear any crap about Job, or what anyone else in the Bible suffered, like Father Hogg tried to tell me the first time I went to see him. Me, Timmy, Katie, Ellen—we ain't in the Bible. None of us are any sorts of prophets or holy men. You're not gonna find us talking in tongues down the supermarket; trying to convert people at the laundromat. What the Hell you making an example of us for?

I was wiping myself when I heard the knock at the door. I figured one of the volunteers must've left something behind. But when I went down, Shirley was standing on the porch. "I just come over to sponge a drink," she said.

I shut the door.

She moved to the window, tapped on it with her knuckles. "Hey, c'mon. It's cold out here."

"It ain't that cold," I said, sitting on the couch, but not turning to look at her.

"All right, it's hot then."

I fought not to smile.

"Look, it don't have to be nothing special. Food coloring. Lime after shave. Anything with alcohol."

"Go away."

"C'mon, Jim is driving me crazy. Us broads got to stick together. I thought we could burn a couple of bras together." She banged on the glass. "C'mon, you thick Mick meatball."

I closed my eyes. I didn't want to laugh, but she used to call me that when we were teenagers, because I was kind of round and short. I called her the Czech dumpling because she was so long and lumpy. The nicknames became secret passwords to let each other know, when we met in the corridors at school, how our dates had gone that weekend. "Did he eat any dumplings?" I might ask her. "Did he make any meatballs?" she'd ask me.

"C'mon Pat, I feel like a peeping Tom. Either let me in, or do something kinky to yourself."

"I'm not letting you in."

"Hey, look, I admit I'm an asshole. Why else would I be friends with an asshole like you? But us assholes have to stick together. Who else will put up with us?"

I was still angry at her, sure. More, I was angry at myself for not feeling like I could tell her I was sorry. I knew, if I let her in, we'd both have to apologize. I wanted to. But I just didn't feel I could. Who the hell knows why? Maybe it was because I'd done nothing but fight with everyone these last six years just to get treated with a little respect, and I wasn't about to back down here. I felt like I was making a stand. It was a stupid place to make a stand. But I've always been thick-headed.

"I got a new *Playgirl*," she said. She pressed the magazine to the glass, opened at the centerfold. "We can get all hot looking at it and go cruising. Pick us up a couple of stud winos."

I stood up and actually started running towards the stairs. She raised her voice loud to yell, "Hey? Pat! Don't try to run away, you know I'll catch you." I kept on moving, even though I knew she was right.

I stood in Katie's room, as I had so many nights after everyone was asleep. Just stood and stared. I wasn't looking for anything so much as just remembering what she'd lost. The quick grin on her face. That sly, mischievous look in her eyes when she was planning something out. She was always so independent. I guess because of what Shirley said, I thought of that you-can't-stop-me look Katie used to sometimes wear. Whenever I saw that look, I couldn't help but hold my breath. Usually it meant Katie was plotting out a way to run off.

Some kids, they won't go nowhere. I could put Ellen in the middle of downtown Pittsburgh and come back three days later and she'd still be standing in the same spot. But when Katie was little, if I so much as turned my back she'd scoot. I'd be frantic, running around the neighborhood, looking for her; screaming her name, my heart beating under my ribs like it might shake all my bones loose. Shirley was the one who was good at finding her hiding place—behind some bushes, or beneath a chair on a neighbor's porch. When Shirley brought Katie back to me, Katie would be laughing. "It's not funny," I'd say, and I'd wallop her behind. And when she'd start crying I'd feel so bad because, well, she's your kid, and before I spanked her she was happy. It don't help much to know what you did was right when you see how miserable you've made them.

The worst time was once when we went on vacation to the beach. We'd gotten a little cottage in one of those summer towns full of bungalows crammed no more than two feet apart. I was pregnant with Ellen, and after the drive I had to go to the bathroom so bad I practically broke the cottage door down. Timmy had his arms full of suitcases, trying to get it all inside as quickly as he could, and I guess he thought I was watching Katie. I thought he was. We hadn't said nothing to each other. When I finished and flushed, I came out into the shaded, sandy-floored den and said, "Where's our good girl?"

Timmy started to smile, then it was like his face fell, there was that kind of movement to it. "I thought she was with you."

"Don't worry, I'm sure she's here. Katie?" I checked the two bedrooms. It was like Timmy's arms went stiff, the way he released the baggage and it tumbled down to the floor.

FAITH IN WHAT?

"Katie?" I called, my voice more anxious. "Katie honey?" Timmy yelled, his voice, like it always does when he's feeling stress, pinched and high.

I checked the house twice while he ran outside and circled our cottage, then the ones next door. I listened to his voice calling her name from all directions, a volley of pleas, as if he were trying to surround us, flush her out with his concern. It was 1:18 on a Saturday afternoon, the narrow streets full of cars and people all the way from our cottage to the beach, nearly a mile away.

Timmy came in, frantic, his face looking like one of those people you see on TV who lived in a concentration camp. "Pat," he said.

"Hold on, just wait, she has to be around," I told him.

We decided I should stay, in case she came back, and he would search the area, working in circles. It was an idea I remembered from LASSIE. I didn't know if it was a good or bad idea, but it was the only thing I could think of. I waited until Timmy left before I let myself cry, a short, hard spasm of tears, more like I was puking something up than sobbing. Then I wiped my face and, even though it was in the eighties, and I was seven months pregnant, I walked around and around the cottage without stopping, calling Katie's name.

It was a beach community. Tourists. Nobody who knew anybody else. Timmy, besides having the look of a fugitive from not having shaved, was probably the only person in the entire place wearing dungarees—he always had a thing about wearing shorts, as if only sissies showed their legs. To the other people there, he probably looked more like a child molester than a distraught father. I realize this now, looking back. But at the time, when he couldn't get anybody else to help him look, I felt like I could take a machine gun and shoot down the whole bunch. Actually, he did find some helpers. Nearly a dozen children, between six and ten years of age, joined the search. But it soon became apparent they were dragging other little girls from the beach to see if they were the Katie Timmy was looking for. He had to tell them to stop.

Of course, we tried the police. They said it was too early to report a missing child—you had to wait twelve hours—and, anyways, they were so short-staffed they couldn't do much more than write it up and keep an eye out.

Every half hour Timmy came back to the cottage to check, his face distorted with such desperate hope I wanted to lie to him. But I'd shake my head before he even reached the yard and he'd turn, without a word, his small shoulders hunched, his head bowed, as if he were begging God or something. At first I thought, she's lost. Then, maybe she got hit by a car. After a while, I began to imagine station wagons pulling beside her, doors opening, gnarled hands dragging her inside. I thought I could deal with anything but that.

Finally, I went inside the cottage for a glass of water. "Jesus, what have I done to deserve this?" I demanded to know. "Give her back to me." I stood at the bathroom sink, looking at my face in the mirror. It terrified me—not so much because of the fear which showed itself in my eyes, which were glassy and wet and wouldn't stop moving. But because it seemed like I had two faces. One, my visible face, was a sort of heavy, rounded rectangle that went with the rest of my body. This was the Pat everyone knew, the jolly, loud-mouthed Pat who wasn't afraid of nothing. Hidden beneath this face, just hinted at, it seemed, by the pug button of my nose, my narrow, worried mouth, and those same, skittering eyes, was the face of someone I might have been, a smaller person in every way. It was like the difference between realities and possibilities, what was there, and a kind of glimmer of what might be there, or might not. Like there was someone hiding inside me that I'd never known about.

Then, even though it was my face I was looking at, I started to see this image of Katie's face, in black and white, on a poster. Missing. If we found her, things would be normal again. But if she never came back...I couldn't imagine what my life would be like, what would be left of me, if that happened.

I was calling her name again before I made it out to the porch.

"What, Mumma?" came a reply.

She was sitting in the dirt behind the station wagon, playing with two popsicle sticks that, I saw when I ran to her, were still damp from the melted ice. "Where have you been?" I asked.

"Right here," she said, and she giggled.

I could get nothing more out of her. I was never able to find out. I hugged her then until she squirmed, wanting to be let go. Looking at her, relief washed down on me like a cleansing force. Then I felt it turning, darkening to anger at the grief she'd put me through. My arms tensed, my hands made fists. I was shocked to feel how quickly heartache could turn to anger. I don't know what I would've done if Timmy hadn't returned.

"Katie?" he said, disbelieving his eyes. "Is that you, honey?"

She looked briefly at him, smiling, then returned to her drawing game on the ground.

I'd never seen a man weep before. This is Steel City, after all. But Timmy dropped to his knees and scooped Katie tight and even when she pushed at him and started whining to be let go, he held on. The tears came so hard and fast from his face it was like the flesh inside his body was pouring out. "Don't ever go away like that again," he said when he eventually released her.

Katie gave him one of her petulant looks, rolled her eyes. "I didn't go away, you did," she said. She stood, brushed her hands off, and ran to the cottage door. "Can I get my bathing suit on?"

Timmy's face, streaked with tears and dirt, looked beautiful to me—there was so much joy in his eyes. I waved Katie forward. The screen door banged behind her and I turned to Timmy. "We got our baby back," he said.

I felt guilty then, for all the anger I had inside. Seeing Timmy made me realize how lucky we were to have her, how at any minute something could happen you had no control over. Of course, when Katie took sick I thought back on this day and wondered if it were a test run of some sort, to see if we could handle it. And, of course, that made me think we should've done a worse job, we should've pulled our hair out and lay down and beat our fists on the ground. Failed the test.

But that day, I took Timmy's face in my hands and gave him a kiss on the mouth. He pulled me toward him, his arm going around my shoulders. I snaked my arm around his waist. I tipped my head onto his shoulder; he tipped his to top mine. We walked into the cottage, and I never felt more lost, but in a good way—like none of us were separate people anymore, but part of this one thing, this family. It was like we'd been tested, and had passed; like God had given us a trial, and now that it was over, nothing bad would ever happen to us again. We had proven ourselves worthy. We had held together through it all. Ellen gave a kick then, and I felt that sharp pain under my ribcage as a promise of grace.

Now, downstairs, Shirley was pounding on the door, calling to be let in. The noise brought me back to this room, the rough boards of the railing, to Katie, who might never run anywhere again.

"Leave me alone Shirl'," I said softly. "I just want to be sad."

As if she heard me, Shirley responded with a howl like a hound hunting something down. "Aaaooooowww," she called. "You're not going to get away from me forever."

Chapter 8

THE CAR wouldn't start. Timmy shook the steering wheel, then looked back at Gerry's apartment. As he watched, the blinking lights framing Gerry's windows stopping flashing. Then the whole apartment went dark. It was just as well, he thought. He didn't really want to go back there for help. That last conversation had made Timmy uneasy. All the talk about not getting any help, and taking what you needed—the moment Gerry said it, it was like he'd unleashed thoughts and feelings that Timmy had been harboring, without knowing it. I mean, Timmy thought, what the hell are people supposed to do? You got to live. And as far as he could see into the future, if you wanted to even call it a future, there was nothing for him, not even the least little bit of hope.

He idly looked through his windshield at the muted silver lines and curves the streetlamps painted on the tops and sides of the cars along the road. Well, what was he going to do now, sit in the car all night? If Pat hadn't had it out with Shirley he could call Jim.

Thinking about it, Timmy pictured himself dialing a phone, explaining his situation. He saw Jim, who'd been Timmy's friend since before first grade, nodding on his end. Jim's mouth would widen into that easy, catlike grin. He'd run his long fingers across his angular, receding forehead, half-pull, half-comb through the red curls on the back of his head. Jim would tell him, "Be there quicker than you can shake your dick."

"Quicker than *you* can shake my dick," Timmy would banter.

"You wish," Jim would say, giving out one of those goofy, bouncing laughs of his. He'd be there in minutes, doing something to make Timmy laugh so all this other stuff wouldn't seem so bad. If Pat hadn't called. If...

Yeah, well, so what 'if'? Timmy told himself. There wasn't no if. Pat had called and that was that. As Timmy's father used to say, "You shit on your plate, you eat it."

In the car, zipping up his sweatshirt against the cold, Timmy felt like he'd been doing a lot of shit-eating lately. Problem was, he didn't feel like it was his shit to begin with.

He looked around at all the cars, their owners probably all asleep. It was a long way to the Vale from this neighborhood of Highland Park. He considered stealing a car. Back in junior high, the guys would often steal a car on weekend nights. But Timmy had been just a rider. He'd never hotwired an ignition. He didn't even know how.

He decided to see if he could find a bus, when a high-pitched laugh startled him. He slunk low in his seat, not wanting whoever it was to see him. A young couple strolled past, their strides languorous, yet somehow excited. Timmy lifted his face to see better. They turned in two houses down, walked up the front steps, and stopped on the porch outside the door. The girl shook her long hair as she gave a quick glance up and down the street, then she pulled the boy's face to hers and they started kissing. His hands went inside her black, wide-lapelled jacket, to her breasts, then travelled down to caress her legs, squeeze her buttocks through the tight leather of her skirt. She rubbed him in the crotch, pulled him tight with the other arm, which was around his waist. Breaking off the kiss, she quickly squatted, her hands working on the boy's zipper.

"What are you doing?" the boy asked in an urgent, embarassed whisper. His searched the streets. Seeing no one, he turned back to the grinning girl.

She pressed her face to his crotch. Timmy watched her head move back and forth. He became aroused, watching, though he couldn't really see anything. It was the idea of it, the thought of that kind of bold intimacy. He felt ashamed at himself for watching, for getting a thrill out of it. Then he felt bitter towards Pat. If it wasn't for her, Timmy told himself, he wouldn't be doing this. They used to share such moments of wild, crazy excitement. But in the last few years, he'd had to practically beg her to sleep with him. Forget everything else. Those rare times when she relented to his advances, Timmy felt like a rapist. She'd just lay there, showing no response, turning her mouth from his kisses, keeping her hands to the bed. When he finished, she'd either roll onto her side, away from him, or get right up and go downstairs to watch TV. And those times were so infrequent, often separated by months, that Timmy had stopped thinking about her, what she might like, and become selfish. Whenever the opportunity came up, he felt he had to rush through it while he had a chance. Before she changed her mind.

There was no longer any sense of tenderness between them. That was one more thing that had been taken from him. Thinking about it, Timmy told himself, I might as well be with a prostitute. Actually, a prostitute might be better. She might at least smile, pretend she was happy to be with him, put her arms around his back and hug him. It couldn't be any worse than what he was doing now.

To feelings of disgrace, he'd begun masturbating again. He, a married man. Of all his troubles, that seemed the greatest source of humiliation. What made it worse, was that he never had the house to himself, so he had to find moments of privacy—while Ellen was at school and Pat in the cellar with volunteers, or when he was alone with Katie and could leave her in her room for a few minutes while he slipped into the bathroom. He'd rush through it, finding no joy, only the diminished pressure which came with the release. Finished, he'd be assailed by feelings of failure, worthlessness. What kind of man was he? Thirty-three years old, married with two kids, jerking off in the bathroom. Even though he'd wash himself two or three times, and spray air freshener about the room, he worried, too, that the heavy, bleach-like smell of his sperm hung upon him like a judgement.

He didn't understand how his life had become so reduced.

He tried to figure it out as he locked up his car and started walking down the tilted sidewalks towards the bus stop. From the first, Pat had been aggressive, enthusiastic. He'd met her back in high school. He, Jim, and a boy named Frank Correnti were standing at the corner of Murray and Forbes, in Squirrel Hill. On weekends, all the kids with cars would cruise back and forth on Forbes, making a one block loop in either direction. Those without cars, like Timmy and his friends, would stand on the corners, watching for carloads of girls to go by. It was a warm night in late April. Timmy, Jim, and Frank were all tanked up on rum and coke Frank's brother-in-law, Chip Metcalfe, had bought for them, and let them drink in John's used bookstore, Cottage Booksmith, which Frank told them was just a front for a bookie operation. The boys were laughing, staggering more than they needed to, punching each other on the arms and whistling any time a carload of girls went by. A station wagon pulled to a halt at the light and three girls jumped out, leaving their doors open. They ran around the car in a game known, for no explicable reason, as Chinese firedrill. It was like musical chairs, with the girls jumping in whatever door they were beside when the light changed back to green.

They were typical Pittsburgh girls. Two of them were tall, with dark wavy hair and strong features, full-breasted in a way that hinted at future heaviness. The third girl was Pat. She was already overweight, stumpy and squat, with small breasts and straight hair cut in a short, boyish fashion.

"Dibs on the driver," Jim said, and he ran through the running circle of girls and dove into the front seat.

"I hosey the one in red," Frank called, referring to the other tall one, who wore a red sweater. He scrambled into the back.

That left Timmy and Pat. Timmy was uncertain. It wasn't that he thought he was too good for her. He'd never even kissed a girl, yet, and the idea of being in a car with any girl excited him. But he was afraid his friends would make fun of her, and he was trying to balance his desires against his need not to be laughed at.

The light changed. Horns honked. The girl in the red sweater told the driver, "Move."

Pat stepped forward, grabbed Timmy's arm, and yanked him in after her. "C'mon dummy," she said. She was joking, but Timmy caught a slight defensiveness in her tone.

Everyone in the car laughed as Timmy tumbled inside, sprawling over Pat, Frank, and the girl in red.

"Jeez," Pat said, looking at Timmy. "What are you, from Cleveland? Duh, what's a red light?" Everyone laughed harder. Timmy pretended to be drunker than he was, to be oblivious to her comments. He let her push him up to a seated position, feeling a cheap thrill as his head brushed across her breasts.

"There, now you sit there like a good boy," Pat told him, setting his hands on his knees. After a second she added,"Well, not too good."

"Pat!" the driver said, flashing a smile over her shoulder. Jim slid across the seat towards her.

"Don't be a girl," the driver said, "Push over."

"But I am a girl," Jim said in falsetto. "A good girl." He made odd motions with his head, moving it back and forth, mimicking shyness as he sang a verse from the Tubes' song, "Don't Touch Me There." The girls howled.

"We've got some rum," Frank said. He pulled from inside his jacket a half pint of Bacardi.

"Thank you," Pat said, snapping it from his hand. Her girlfriend in the back seat laughed. Pat gulped from the bottle and looked at Timmy. "Don't think you can get me drunk and take advantage of me." she gulped. "You don't need to get me drunk." She was the only one who laughed. She gulped some more. She leaned forward, passing the bottle to the driver. "This is the type of guy I like. A talker."

Timmy lolled his head against the window. Everyone was laughing again and he didn't know how he could be a part of it.

He felt like saying, Screw you you fat cow, you ain't no bargain either. But he knew if he said anything, Frank and Jim would be mad at him for ruining their chances.

"You know what they say," Pat told her girlfriends, "Small mouth, big..."

"Pat!" The girl in back reached around Frank to punch Pat on the arm.

"Pat what?" Pat said. "I was gonna say big ears." Pat turned to Timmy and brushed the hair back over his ears. Her fingers were small and thick, but they moved gently. "See? A regular Dumbo." She winked at Timmy. "Just kidding," she said. She brushed at his hair for a few more seconds. No one had ever done that, and Timmy didn't want her to stop. "Soft," she said quietly.

"He's soft?" Frank said in mock horror.

Jim turned around in the seat. He affected a gay accent and said, "I just wore him out."

Pat threw her arms around Timmy and said to Jim, "I'll fight you for him."

Timmy was thrilled at the feel of her arms, the herbal odor of her shampoo. The silkiness of her hair as it brushed his chin excited and terrified him. With hope and disgust he thought, she must put out! He looked at Jim, seeking guidance. Jim made a slight punching motion, Go for it. In a deadpan voice, Timmy managed to say, "May the best man win."

Pat said, "The great god speaks!" They all laughed because Timmy had broken his silence. Pat leaned forward, challenged Jim, "Well let's go. Whip it out. We'll see who's got the biggest weenie."

This time, everyone was embarassed. Timmy was incredulous. Girls said anything these days, but still. There was a tension in the car which could've meant the end of the ride, but Jim said, "I always leave mine at home when I'm going out with strangers."

They ended up at the drive-in that night. Timmy was ⌐ at how quickly Pat let him kiss her with his mouth open then let him slip his hand inside her bra. It was his first time. He didn't know quite what to do with her breast. He gave it a few squeezes, then flicked the nipple back and forth with his fingertip. She was the one who suggested they slide over the back seat into the rear storage area.

The windows were completely fogged, the car full of the dry, husky sounds of breathing, the slipping, smacking sounds of lips, and a sort of rhythmic, squishing sound he later learned came from Jim and the girl in the front seat.

Pat opened her blouse for Timmy, unsnapped her bra herself. Timmy stared, unsettled at the sight of her erect nipples. Pat took his head and guided it so that his mouth was on her. Timmy sucked her breast inside his lips and began chewing. "Easy," she said in a sharp whisper which made the car quiet momentarily. Timmy felt like a fool. He pulled his head back. Pat forced it down again. "Just go easy, they ain't made of rubber," she said.

This time, Timmy licked her breasts broadly with the flat of his tongue, as if he were licking an ice cream cone. When he tired of that, he took them in his hands and squeezed them the way he'd seen a farmer milking a cow in a filmstrip at school. He half-expected to see milk come from them, was surprised when it didn't. Holding on, as if he feared, were he to let go, she would take them away from him, Timmy slid up and pressed his mouth so hard against Pat's mouth, it hurt. He shook her breasts like marocas. She smiled at him. "Are you having fun?" "Yeah," he told her uncertainly, starting to pull back again. She held him fast with her arm and told him, "Me too," before pressing her mouth to his.

He didn't know what to do next, how to go on to the next stage. I'm on second base, he told himself, but how do I get to third? He was afraid to try something, for fear she would stop him, and then what would he do?

It was Pat who took his hand, finally, and slipped it inside the tight band of her pants, and beneath her girdle. It took Timmy nearly half a movie to work his hand down to where it belonged.

When he did, she moaned, and he stopped, out of fear the others might hear. But she stroked his forearm and he kept wiggling his fingers around.

By the time the second movie started, Timmy's arm was numb and tingling. What did she want from him next? he wondered. The first touch of Pat's fingers in his crotch made him jump.

She gave a soft, nearly silent, laugh in his ear, then blew in there, flicked her tongue inside and he shivered. His zipper made a loud scratching sound as she pulled on it, but she never hesitated. She clutched Timmy through his underwear and he came so fast the spasms made his groin jerk. He moved like a fish, bottom half flopping, his left arm numb and trapped inside her girdle. He was so sensitive, even her hand through the cloth hurt him. But he grit his teeth, squeezed his eyes shut, and accepted the pain.

After that, he saw her every day. She had so many ideas, he felt like she must've invented sex. He felt like no one had ever experienced it with the intensity they did. They found places to do it—grassy hillsides behind abandoned factories; cars, whose windows they broke to enter, on dealers' lots after the lots closed for the day; houses under construction, open frames dusted with sawdust and charged with the threat of discovery; and, of course, the parks and wooded areas which were everywhere around them. One time they squeezed into the storage area for rubbish barrels beneath her parents' outside stairway and Pat moaned so loudly her father came out to see if someone were in his yard.

A number of times they went, after dark, to the beer warehouse, where trailer trucks loaded with kegs were backed to the locked steel doors, waiting to be unloaded the next morning. There was just enough space between the warehouse and the truck's doors for Timmy and Pat to crawl inside and find a dark space of privacy amid the silver barrels and sour stench of beer.

When it became apparent he was serious about her, it was Jim who started talking, when Timmy and his friends got together, about how funny Pat was, and how she had a good personality, a cute face. Timmy was thankful for Jim's help—no one asked Timmy about the sex after that—although he felt bad about some of the things he'd said before to the guys about Pat, what she'd done to him, and the fact that he hadn't had the courage to admit he liked her. She *was* funny, and she *was* considerate, always asking about him, how he felt, and telling him—Don't listen to your father, he's an asshole. Timmy enjoyed being with her more than with anyone he'd ever known, even Jim.

Shortly after he graduated, Timmy got a job at the plant. A year later he and Pat were married in a church. They went to the Jersey shore for their honeymoon, and came back to their first apartment. It was like they were starting at the beginning again. They'd never had rooms of their own to have sex in. They felt like kids who'd been left alone by their parents, without supervision, and so could indulge all their fantasies without anyone ever finding out. The fact that they were married, too, and could legally do anything, made Timmy feel even more unrestrained.

And when their passion wore down, they were still people who touched and held each other, gave back rubs and foot massages, brushed one another's hair. Then Katie came along

From the first, Timmy was filled with awe and wonder at this new life. He and Pat would sit together at night, once Katie was asleep, and shake their heads, they felt so blessed. "What did we do to deserve this?" Pat asked. For Timmy, it was like chambers in his heart were opening up, chambers he'd never guessed existed. He was stunned by what he felt was his increased capacity for love.

When Ellen came along, rather than taking some of that from him, he felt his love increasing even more. There were times at night when he would wake up in a sweat from some nightmare where his kids had been stolen from him, or lost, and Pat would hold Timmy and rock him and tell him, "I get so afraid too, but we can't kill ourselves with worrying." "I never knew love could be so dangerous, so terrifying," Timmy said. He knew he would do anything for his kids—jump in front of cars, cut off his own legs, kill, really kill, anyone who tried to harm them. "I was never afraid of dying before," he told Pat one night. "But I am now. Not for me. I want to live long enough to see them grow up, to hold Katie's babies, and see Ellen's kids learn how to talk."

"Wait until they're teenagers, and you'll probably want to kill them yourself," Pat said. "What are you gonna do when they start doing the things we did?"

"Oh Jesus," Timmy said, and they both laughed. Then they'd roll together, make love, not worrying about birth control, opening themselves to the risk of pregnancy as if to affirm the joy in their lives.

He made a simple life for himself, and he was happy with it. He had a job, a wife, a family, buddies at work. For the first time, he felt he really belonged somewhere. Like there was a point to his living. The whole of his life was like a huge bubble, expanding as it rose above the world. Maybe it was sentimental, he thought, but he told himself, This is how stars are made. He envisioned Pat, Katie, Ellen and himself, standing in a circle with their arms around each other, floating into the night sky to become another distant, contented pinpoint of light. Nothing special. Nothing out of the ordinary. Just another pulsing glow among the millions.

Then, Katie. Her illness was a fist that punched the air out of him. Everything deflated, folded in, hardened. Soon after Katie's problems, the plant shut down, Pat shrivelled away, even Ellen grew distant, guarded her affections as if they were precious and limited. Perhaps she felt Timmy's uncertainty. Now that Ellen was six, the same age as Katie when Katie took ill, Timmy had begun to fear the same might happen to her that had happened to her older sister. He felt himself pulling away from her against his will. It was as if he wanted to create some distance, in case it did happen again, so it wouldn't hurt as much.

And in this whole mess, he had somehow lost Pat. They had lost each other. It was like he'd lost everything, and he didn't know where to start getting things back.

Timmy looked around now, temporarily disoriented. He'd

been walking through the city without paying any attention to where he was going, so lost was he in thought. Apparently, he'd made it through East Liberty and into Squirrel Hill. He was at the intersection where he'd first met Pat. That unsettled him even more. If I could go back, he thought, just for a few minutes, get that feeling all over again. He thought about that first night with Pat, at the drive-in. He thought about the girl kneeling on the porch across from Gerry's place. He wanted so much just to be able to feel like that again.

To his left, three skateboard punks raced through the deserted parking lot beneath the library. Across the street, to the right of the Gulf station, the Jewish Community Center, an impressive brick structure as large as a temple, seemed to shine, although there weren't any lights on it. You never heard of Jews being unemployed, he thought. What was their secret?

He was sick of thinking about jobs, of worrying. He wanted some diversion to take his mind away from it all. He crossed the street and headed down the steep slope of Murray Avenue. At the bottom, he could pick up the Parkway out of town. If he thumbed, maybe someone would give him a ride home. Home, to cold sheets, Pat on the couch pretending to be asleep. Another night staring at the ceiling.

He passed pizza shops, bakeries. An Eat 'n Park restaurant was open. Three elderly men sat at the counter. Timmy found himself wondering—could you really rob a place like this and get away with it? C'mon man, get ahold of yourself, he thought, is this really what you want? I don't know about want, he thought, but I need...something.

He passed more restaurants, grocery stores. All these places for food, expensive places, for people to get anything they wanted while he had to shuffle down to a food pantry and beg for a bag of no-name canned goods. He felt anger and resentment. What had happened to this country? He had voted for Reagan, like all the guys, and now everything seemed to have gone to hell.

He was tired of everything. No jobs, no money, no help. How long could a man go, getting nothing he needed, before something had to give?

Two-thirds of the way down the hill, he spotted, across the street, a lit doorway in the chimney-like wall of a tan brick building whose ground floor was taken up by a kosher butcher shop. The single bulb in the interior behind the door highlighted a red, carpeted staircase leading up. There was a small sign above the door frame: Massage. He looked to the second floor. A heavy drape concealed what lay behind a pair of sliding glass windows. The drape was opened a crack, and a warm, yellow light flowed out. As Timmy watched, a woman's fingers curled around the drape, parted it slightly. A face was barely visible before the drape fell shut.

Oh man, Timmy thought, don't do this to me, but visions of himself going home, locking himself in the bathroom, plagued his mind. Then he remembered the emergency money hidden in his wallet. Money he'd been hoping to save for Christmas. As he stood, looking at the door across the street, everything darkened around him. It was as if he'd fallen into a black hole which was sucking away all the light.

He crossed the street, pretending he was just interested in reading the signs on the butcher shop window; Fresh dressed chicken, veal chops, liver. He discovered he was sweating, and wiped his face on his sweatshirt. He imagined hands touching him, rubbing his back, his face, stroking his hair, cradling his shoulders, pulling him against a fragrant chest and rocking him gently. He took a step backwards, onto the sidewalk. He looked around, but spotted not a single person who might witness him. Oh no, he told himself as he stepped forward to open the door.

The air was stiff and sour smelling. The carpeting had been worn black in the center of the stairs. First his legs were shaking, then he was trembling all over. A coldness spasmed in his gut. I'm not doing anything wrong, he told himself. It's not my fault. I just want someone to touch me.

He stood before a scarred, plywood door. Pop music softly played inside. As he shifted his feet, the floor gave out a low creak. He looked down the staircase. No one was coming up. He turned back to the door, took his hands out of his pockets, then put them back in again. He shifted, cringing at the squeak. He hadn't decided what to do when the door pulled open.

A thin woman with short hair smiled at him, her teeth full, but stained with nicotine. Her eyebrows had been shaved off and drawn back on with eyeliner in a series of sticklike slashes. She wore pink shorts that rode so high the cheeks of her ass showed. A loose midriff T-shirt that said Steelers flopped against the sharp nipples of her small breasts. "You coming in hon'?" She asked. "Don't be shy, I won't bite you." She seemed amused by him. "C'mon. I'm always extra nice to the last customer of the night."

"I don't want to do nothing wrong," Timmy said, turning his face aside in embarassment at having said that.

She laughed, wiped her fingers down her shirt, perking her nipples up a bit, and set her hands on her hips. "Now who ever said there's something wrong in getting rid of a little tension, huh? We all need to treat ourselves sometimes, hon. And you look like..." She looked him over, gave him a smile and a wink. "You look like a man who knows what he needs." She reached forward for his arm and took a quick peek at her watch.

Chapter 9

I'D BEEN DREAMING that I was inside an unfinished house, the frame put up, but the roof missing. The walls were wooden skeletons and I was waiting for someone to come finish the work. I knew, too, that no one would show up, but I had to stay there and wait. When I first heard the voice, it became part of my dream, as those things do. "Mumma, it's time to get me ready." In my dream, I looked down in my lap and there was Katie, hanging from me by an umbilical cord. She was just an infant, but she was wearing the blue sailor dress with the red and white collar she'd worn her first day of school. "Mumma!" she said again and I knew by the rasp of exasperation it wasn't Katie, and I wasn't dreaming the words.

Gunk was so thick in my eyes it felt like they'd been glued shut. I swore I heard a smacking sound when I pulled them open. Ellen stood beside the couch, staring down at me, her small mouth closed, severe. She had on the same outfit she'd worn the day before, the green plaid skirt and white blouse.

I pushed aside the blanket and swung my feet to the rug. "You can't wear that."

"I can't reach the cereal, Daddy put it up on the top shelf and you don't want me to climb on the counter." Her words accused me of idiocy.

"Don't be smart," I said. I looked around. The smoky blue light I usually saw when I got up was already gone. The room was full of a light brown haze. It made the furniture seem older, more worn. "What time is it?"

"You have to write me a note again. I'm going to miss first period."

"Why didn't you get me up earlier?" I stood so quickly my head spun. I thought I was going to faint. Then I remembered we had volunteers coming that morning, at nine—they'd had to switch because a couple of them were busy in the afternoon. "Oh Jeez," I said. "I got to ret up the house, get Katie ready; she needs a bath, and dressed, and hair washed." I headed for the stairs.

"Mumma, my cereal," Ellen said.

"Stop yelling at me," I told her, raising my hands near my ears as if trying to knock her words away. I hurried to the kitchen, climbed the stepstool so I could reach the cereal down from the cabinet above the stove, and put that, and a bowl, onto the table. "You can get the milk yourself," I said as I left. "Your father can give you a ride to school."

At the top of the stairs, just before I turned into Katie's room, I yelled at the closed door of the room I thought of now as Timmy's bedroom, "How about a little help with Ellen?"

Katie was laying in bed, her eyes unblinking, sucking on her hand. "How's my big girl?" I said. When I bent closer I noticed the unreal shine to her pupils, as if she'd just had a startle reaction. Not another, I thought. "You go dying on me and I'll kill you," I told her. I was hoping it wasn't because we'd been cutting her medicine in half, because I didn't see what else we could do. We had to pay for it ourselves, and we couldn't afford to give her a full dose, not at forty bucks a month. It was either cut it in half, or give it to her until it ran out and let her go two weeks with nothing. I untied the ropes, then slid the railing out and set it in the corner, beside Katie's bureau.

We have an upstairs wheelchair, not much more than a rickety metal frame given to us by an ex-volunteer whose mother used it until she died from Alzheimer's. But it was good enough to wheel Katie from her bedroom to the bath. When you rolled it close it was almost level with the mattress, so it was easy to lift her to a seated position and slide her into the seat. I checked first, and was relieved to see she didn't have a mess to be changed. Thank God for small favors. Then I undressed her and set her in the wheelchair to bring her to the bathroom.

When she was first home, me and Timmy bathed her together. Every day we sat her up in the tub, taking turns, one of us holding her, the other cleaning her with a face cloth. Lately, though, we'd been getting lazy. At least I had. I figured he was doing the same as me, although I never asked. It was one of those things you didn't want to know. I'm sure most people would look down on me for it, think I wasn't being a good parent. But it's easy to judge when you don't have someone like Katie to take care of every minute of your life.

This is the way I cleaned her these days. I didn't move her from the chair, just tucked a towel under her bum, and soaped her up while she sat there. It was so much easier; no lifting, no bending, no worry about her sliding under the water. I could clean her off one part at a time. Even her hair. I'd back the wheelchair to the sink and push her head back until it rested on the rim, her hair hanging in the bowl. Sometimes she complained, moaned sort of, and tried to lift her face forward. It was no trouble holding her still, shampooing her up, then rinsing her with water from a cup. I was careful not to use our drinking cup.

The only hard part was...down there, that whole area. But if I pulled her arm over my neck, I could lift her by standing and get the face cloth in there for a few good swipes.

When I was done, I covered her front with a yellow bath towel whose edges were frayed. I wheeled her back to her room, telling her, "Katie..." I was trying to keep my voice cheerful, to say something about the day ahead, like the way you try to get your kids excited by saying you're going to the library, or the playground, or visiting. But I couldn't think of nothing to say. What was I supposed to tell her? Today we're gonna drag you across the floor and make you scream?

"I need you to give me a hand before you drive Ellen to school," I said, opening Timmy's door. The room was empty, the bed already made. Where could he have gone this early? I thought, Don't tell me he got a job. He didn't say nothing to me, but I wasn't too easy to talk to yesterday. And maybe he was planning on surprising me. I tried not to think about it, but I was so excited I carried Katie down the stairs myself. I sort of slung her over my shoulder and bounced her butt on the stairs to take the weight off me. Oh God, I prayed, don't give me this hope if You don't mean it. If Timmy was gone, what else could it be? But if he did have a job, that would mean he couldn't give Ellen a ride to school.

I lay Katie back on the stairs, her head against the wall, while I grabbed her wheelchair. I shifted her into that and pushed her into the kitchen. Ellen was gone. "Damn you," I muttered. If she'd eaten, she hadn't bothered to use a bowl, or milk. What did they think of me down at her school? I wondered as I poured Cheerios and milk into a bowl for Katie. What kind of mother did they think I was? "I'm doing the best I can," I said aloud. I was picturing myself answering the polite accusations of the principal, Mr. Reed. I knew all about him. First, because he was the same principal I had, only he was old now, about sixty, and his thick black hair had gone white and was so thin it couldn't hide his bald crown. I also knew all about him from the time I went down there, arguing with him to let Katie go through classes with kids her own age. "Isn't everyone talking about this mainstreaming?" I said.

He pushed his gold-framed glasses higher onto his thin nose, gave me that lipless, sympathetic smile of his. When he touched my arm just above the elbow, and looked down at me with that sickening sympathetic look of his, I wanted to smack him. "We only mainstream those with some potential," he said. "Some possibility of improvement. Excuse me for speaking bluntly."

"Well if she was in class, seeing her old friends might jar her back to being normal. You know, like, when you got amnesia and someone bops you on the head?" It made sense to me. I don't know how many movies I saw where that happened.

85

He looked at the folder containing her medical records from the rehab. "If, at some future date, she exhibits any, shall we say...display of developmental progress, I'll be happy to reassess the situation. Until such time, I can only assume..."

The words cut through my head like saw blades. Exhibits, display, developmental, reassess—what did words like that have to do with my life? I knew I should keep my mouth shut, but I couldn't stop myself. "Don't assume," I said. "Assume makes an ass out of U and me."

He removed his fingers from my arm so gently it was like they dissolved. His pale blue eyes were almost weepy, they were that full of pity. I hated him for that, for not getting angry, for feeling sorry for me. Without losing his smile, he turned to his secretary and asked her to see me out.

The doorbell rang. For a second I was disoriented. I was in front of Katie, when I expected to be behind her, pushing her down the dim school corridor. There was a raised spoon, full of Cheerios, in my hand. Katie's head was craned forward on her neck, her mouth open, as if in blind hope that it might bump against some food. I'm home, I thought. This is today, not some time years ago. I looked at the clock—8:53. The first volunteer, and I hadn't even had my cup of coffee.

Only two people showed up, Alex, a retired man who used to be a weight lifter, and Nina, a beautiful young Italian girl who was in A.A. I felt exhausted before we started, my body achey, as if I'd been beaten with sticks. Anger was like an ugly mask pushing and pulling on the muscles of my face. I couldn't stop my mouth from moving. I bitched about no one showing up, people not caring, not living up to their commitments and responsibilities. "A lot of good this does me," I said. "Two people. Can't do the program, can't do..." this and that, bitch bitch bitch, blah blah blah.

Finally, Alex told me, "Pat, that's enough. *We're* here aren't we? Don't take it out on us."

"Yeah, half a crew. That's par for a Tuesday," I said.

"Keep it up and you won't have anybody," he said.

He was holding Katie under the arms, his hands clasped at her chest. Her arms flopped out loosely. I was kneeling on the floor with Nina. We were each controlling one of Katie's feet, taking turns moving them forward in a simulation of walking. I'd just finished yelling at Nina for not pressing the heel flat before bending the toes down.

I felt my shoulders slump at what Alex had said. I lowered my head, wanting to apologize. I couldn't understand. It seemed I was all the time doing things that made me want to apologize, but I could never get myself to do it. It was like I wanted to feel bitter and angry. I wanted to hold onto those feelings, as if they gave me power. As if hurting other people was the only way I could talk about how I hurt inside. Or as if I were punishing God, telling Him, okay, if You're not going to do nothing for me, I'm not going to be nice to others. It made me sick, because I wasn't that type of person. Not really.

The doorbell rang. The sound came as a reprieve. I could go up, answer it, and come back down and start over.

"See?" Nina said. she was already moving towards the bulkhead, to go outside for a cigarette. "Be patient, things work out. That's probably another volunteer."

"You're right," I said. "Sometimes I get so used to things not working out, I almost want them to go bad, so I can feel sorry for myself. But it's crazy, because, you know, I hate it when other people feel sorry for me."

"Well, Pat, who ever said you made sense?" Alex smiled.

I stood up, rubbed at the soreness in my knees. "Yeah? Well, if I don't make sense, and you're down here doing what I tell you, what's that say about you?"

The doorbell rang again. I looked up the stairs.

"Better grab that sucker before he gets away," Alex smiled.

I started up the steps, moving in a slow, tight-legged hobble. "This guy's staying if I have to do the, what's it called, that them belly dancers do? The Dance of the Seven Veils?"

Alex laughed. "Where are you going to get seven veils big enough?"

"Okay," I told him. "So the Dance of the Seven Potato Sacks. But when he sees this body..." I made a clicking sound with my mouth.

When I peeked through the window in the door at the man on the porch, though, the way he looked made me nervous. He had sunken brown eyes that pierced you at a glance, they were that intense. He wasn't that old, but his moustache was a solid gray, like a January sky. His dark hair was streaked with gray, too. It was so thin, jagged lines of his scalp showed through. As I opened the door, I thought he looked unnervingly familiar.

"I lost my key," he said.

"Timmy?" I felt so bad, I turned away. I headed for the kitchen. Over my shoulder I told him, "Just go downstairs, I'll be right down." I went to the sink and covered my hands with pink dish liquid.

"I'm sorry," he said, "I mean..." His footsteps were slow and shuffling as he edged in beside me. Our bodies brushed against each other and I shifted my weight to my left leg, to break contact. I squirted soap into Timmy's cupped palms, then rinsed my hands under the fizzing stream pouring out of the faucet. The round clock above the sink showed that it was 9:35. My body stiffened. It was the weirdest thing. I had a feeling of *deja vu*, like I had been through this all before. Then I remembered. We'd stood side by side like this the day Timmy lost his job at the plant. He'd come home all upset that day. When the guys went to punch out for lunch, their time cards had little slips attached to them. No two weeks notice, no severance pay, no nothing. The offices where the bosses sat were empty, locked.

"We got enough saved until they call you back," I'd told him that time.

"There ain't gonna be no callback," he'd said. "The place is shut for good."

Back then, I hugged him and brought him upstairs to give him a backrub. "This is Pittsburgh. They can't keep a good

Hunky down. You'll find something else. The union will take care of you."

"I guess," he said. His voice, muffled by the pillow, sounded soft, uncertain.

"A big man like you," I told him, turning him onto his back. "Let me check your tools, make sure they're in good working order."

"My socket wrench?" he smiled.

"More like your drill, your screwdriver." He laughed with me as I pulled down his pants and growled, "Your hammer." Then we were on each other like cats.

That seemed so long ago, though. I'd never do nothing like that now. These days, if he even looked like he wanted to touch me I froze. I don't know why. How can you figure these things? Maybe it's because we're always nipping at each other like yappy dogs. I guess it's because I got so many things on my mind, with Katie and all.And what if, anyways, what if...what if it *is* something wrong with me, my genes or something? If we got pregnant and had another kid who turned out like Katie? At church they say you're supposed to open yourself to that kind of risk, but, my God, I was sick enough with worrying about one, and trying to pretend I wasn't terrified the same thing might happen to Ellen at any moment. The thought of doing something that might give me another life to ruin...

I scrunched my shoulder up, so I could rub my eye on it. Beside me, a deep chirping sound came from Timmy's throat. He rinsed his small, thick-muscled hands beneath the faucet, the dark hair glinting like fur at his wrists. "I have to tell you something," he said.

You couldn't miss the sadness, the apology, in his voice. "You didn't get the job," I said.

He looked at me like he thought I was losing it. "What are you talking about?" he asked.

"Just don't worry. My knee feels a little better. I should be able to lug that sample case around again soon. I mean, with Christmas coming, people will be buying Amway like crazy.

Between that and your check, it should carry us through the first of the year."

He tossed his head back. "I can't think about that right now." His voice was so strained, it sounded like it might crack. "It's something else I got to tell you."

He paused and I looked around. "I feel so bad," he said.

I thought I knew what he was getting at. I wasn't sure I wanted to hear it, though, so I told him, "Well, yeah, I do too. How can we not feel bad? I mean, Jesus. I got nothing in my head but 'Katie needs'. Katie needs a special chair, and Katie needs a hanging bar, and..."

"Will you stop it?" He shook his hands in the sink once, hard. "For Chrissakes Pat, forget the damned special things. We gotta straighten out the basics. You and me." He went to rip a paper towel off the roll over the sink and pulled the whole roll down.

"That's what I mean," I said.

"Listen dammit," he said. He snapped the roll back into its plastic holder. Leaning on the front rim of the sink, he stared out the window at our barren, brown yard. "I'm trying to apologize..."

"You don't have to. It's not your fault."

"What are you talking about?"

I pointed at the ceiling, feeling a little confused. "I saw you went out early this morning. Didn't you go to apply for a job?"

"I didn't come home from Gerry's last night," he said. There were tears starting in his eyes. His face darkened to a purplish red.

I figured he felt he'd abandoned us. This was his home. He was supposed to be here. Guarding his castle. All that men stuff. I didn't know if it would be better to tell him no one missed him, or to say nothing. "Well, the game was late, you'd been drinking."

"The car wouldn't start. So I started walking hom;;e..." He paused. His brow was loose and puckered. Thin, deep trenches flared from the sides of his eyes, mouth, and nose. His moustache covered his weak upper lip, the hair as thick as rug pile.

"Oh Timmy, I wouldn't expect you to walk. So you stayed at Gerry's? What's the big deal?"

He shook his head, raised one hand.

"Look, there are volunteers downstairs. We can talk about this later."

"Didn't you ever do anything, and later, when you realized it was a mistake, you couldn't take it back because you'd already done it?"

I didn't have to think for a second about that one. "Oh yeah," I told him. "Oh yeah." I looked past him, through the kitchen, to the living room, at the window where I'd stood and watched him come home the first time he'd been laid off, the day Katie took sick. The day I'd sent her outside.

This is my home. This place full of memories of lay-offs, sickness, hard times, and guilt. I let my eyes drift around, not really focusing on anything, when everything shifted on me. Just slightly, an inch here or there. It was like I'd stepped into a world that was somewhat familiar, but wasn't mine. I looked at the porcelain sink, the formica counters, the cheap wooden cabinets, plywood but stained dark...all of it appeared hollow, like it might shatter if I tapped it too hard with my fingers; and I had this fear, that there was something behind there I didn't want to see.

"Pat," he started. "I have to tell you..." The bulkhead door banged shut. Nina returning to help me put Katie through those endless exercises again.

"I don't have the time right now," I told Timmy. I felt myself being pulled away. It was almost like someone was dragging me physically from him. I was so full of my own problems, I just didn't have the energy to listen to him.

"What I want to know," I said, "is what do people do? Just what do people do in this world? What, dear God, do they do?"

Timmy, his movements abrupt, lunged at me and planted a dry, hard kiss on my cheek. "I love you," he said. His hands shook as he touched my shoulders, tried to jerk his arms around my back to hug me. "I love you, Pat. I love you and the kids." He

91

tried to kiss me again. It nearly broke my heart. I wanted to be able to give in, to hold him and kiss him and cry together. But I couldn't help myself. My body tensed, my muscles went rigid, and I turned my face from his lips so they caught the back of my neck.

He stepped back and gave me a pained look, as if I had betrayed him. But I was already moving beyond him, towards the black, yawning door of the cellar.

Chapter 10

"JESUS LOVES ME," Ellen called over her shoulder. "I don't care what you say because Father Hogg said Jesus and God and the Holy Spirit will always be my friends. And they're better friends than you anyways." She was walking as fast as she could, one arm swinging steadily, her other clutching her books. She didn't want to run. Well, really, she felt like dropping her books and running as fast as she could. But she wasn't going to let them make her run.

Twenty feet behind her, a loose mob of ten to twelve first and second graders followed Ellen, taunting her, occasionally drawing up the courage to pull closer, then losing it and dropping behind. "Cooties, cooties," one girl chanted in a sing-song voice, then several others took up the chant. A tall second-grade boy broke forward, came within a foot of Ellen, reached a hand forth as if to touch her, then, yelling, "Cowabunga," snatched his hand back and hurriedly returned to the group. He wedged himself behind several giggling boys, and they all started pulling and pushing at each other.

Ellen was close to the corner now. she looked up at the streetlight. Cars were passing quickly beneath the bright green disc. Please, God, make the light change, she prayed.

She didn't know if it was the right type of thing to pray for and that made her nervous. What if it was the wrong thing and God got mad and decided to punish her for bothering Him? If He got mad at her, He might not listen to her other prayers, about

Katie getting better. But Ellen was getting tired of asking about that, too. What was taking Him so long? She thought if you asked Him nice and really, really meant it, He would answer you. That's what they told her at cathechism. If you really meant it, God would listen. Only you couldn't ask Him to get you things like My Pretty Pony. But her teacher, Mrs. Steineck, said you could ask for good things to happen to other people. That's what Ellen was asking for for Katie. And she really, really meant it about Katie. Why wasn't God listening to her? She hoped it wasn't because she forgot to pray for Katie sometimes. She hoped God wasn't punishing her for that. She wondered if maybe God was punishing Katie for something bad Katie had done. Thinking about it, wondering what Katie's sin might be, she found herself getting excited.

At the curb, she stopped with her toes poking over the edge. The gutter beneath was full of clotted dirt, cigarette butts, and broken pieces of beer bottles. Yuck, she thought. Why didn't God make people clean up the messes they made? What was He doing up there all day anyways?

She heard a cracking sound and turned. Johnny Nelson, a thin, brown-haired boy with bangs, one of her classmates, was snapping a branch from a sapling in the front yard of an apartment complex. When the other children saw that Ellen was no longer moving, they stopped, ten feet away. Ellen took a step towards them and they shuffled back quickly. Ellen felt good and bad about that, and it made her confused. She hated it when they did this, followed her home in a gang. But at least they were paying attention to her. And she didn't like people being afraid of her, but it was better than being afraid of them.

"Cooties, cooties," sang that same girl. She had on a brand new white blouse and red skirt. There were all kinds of gold bracelets on her arms and she jiggled these. As she sang, the girl tossed her head to make her ponytail swing from side to side.

"You're ugly," called a tow-headed boy. He giggled and elbowed his friends.

"No suh," Ellen said, putting her hands on her hips. She

stamped her foot at them and the children jumped back. "Shows how stupid you are. I'm cute. I have a cute small nose and pretty eyes and when all my teeth are in I'm going to have a nice smile because I use dental floss."

They seemed mystified by her response. No one said anything for a few seconds. Then Johnny Nelson spoke up. "She's not ugly," Johnny Nelson told the boy. "It's just her sister has cooties."

"She does not," Ellen said.

But they didn't pay attention to her, because the girl with the new clothing was telling Johnny, "You're just sticking up for her because you've got a sister who's retarded." Her mouth was small and mean, as set in its expression as a person's whose life has been one long disappointment.

"I do not," Johnny said, his face reddening.

"Do too. That's why my mother said I couldn't be your girlfriend. Because once it's in your family you can't get it out. It stains just like grape juice."

"I don't want you to be my girlfriend," Johnny said.

The girl turned a smug look to the other children. "He asked me last Friday in reading circle. Then my mother told me about his retarded sister."

Johnny's face grew darker. "She's not my sister anymore. My Dad said so. We gave her to the government so she's not my sister anymore."

They were all silent for a moment, wondering about that. Could your parents really do that? Give you to the government? Where would the government put you? Thinking about it, Ellen began to feel really scared. When she noticed that the light had changed, she jumped into the street and started across.

"Hey, she's escaping," someone yelled. There were high-pitched cheers, sounds of hunter-glee, and the group started after her.

Before she reached the opposite sidewalk, Ellen felt a sharp stinging on the back of her legs. She stopped moving, her knees bending involuntarily. The stinging struck again.

"Oww," she said, fighting the urge to cry. She wasn't going to let them see her cry. She turned, her hands held forward, her head bent sideways, for protection.

Johnny Nelson stood several feet in front of the rest of the group. He held the branch pulled back sideways, behind his waist, as he got ready to swing it forward again.

There was a screeching sound of brakes, then one prolonged blare from a car horn. A woman's angry voice yelled, "What the hell you think you're doing?" and everyone froze.

Ellen turned to see a black Delta 88 stopped in the middle of the intersection. The door swung open and Shirley stepped out, a cigarette dangling from the corner of her mouth. Her hair was covered by a purple kerchief and she tugged it down as she stepped forward. Behind her, in the passenger seat, Jimmy Jr. watched with excitement.

The children stood immobile as Shirley grabbed Johnny by the wrist. She ripped the sapling from him, lifted his arm above his head, and spun him so his backside faced her. She snapped the branch twice, rapidly, against his legs. Johnny did a little dance, screeched, and started to cry. "How do *you* like it?" Shirley asked. "You want some more?" She swatted him several more times. He danced and screeched. "What's the matter? Don't you think this is fun?"

The cars jammed behind Shirley's car began to beep their horns. "Blow it out your ass!" she bellowed. The beeping stopped. The sudden indrawn breaths of the children made a low "ooooo" sound.

Shirley still held Johnny, his hands gathered above his head. He was still dancing, crying. She looked at the children, their eyes and mouths widened. "Anybody else think this is fun?" she asked. No one moved. "I see anybody bothering this kid," she motioned at Ellen, "I'll tear the hide off you." She let go of Johnny and swung the branch forward, as if trying to scatter something. The children turned and fled back towards the school, screaming, pushing and jostling to get ahead of each other.

Ellen looked at Shirley, who frowned at the stick and

dropped it in the street. "Get in honey, I'll ride you home," Shirley said.

Ellen glanced over at the car. Jimmy Jr. smiled and waved. Ellen smoothed her skirt, then squinted up at Shirley. "I heard you banging on our door last night," Ellen said.

"If your thick-headed mother had let me in, you wouldn't of heard nothing but us yakking."

"But you don't like us anymore," Ellen said.

Shirley pulled the cigarette from her mouth and exhaled through her nose. "Of course I like you," she said. "Things ain't so cut and dried as they seem sometimes. You know?"

"No," Ellen said.

Shirley looked amused. She looked at the ground briefly, thinking, then turned her eyes on Ellen. "Look. Sometimes things happen and you don't always know what to do. Sometimes you say the wrong thing. Sometimes people say things and it sounds like they hate each other, but that's only because they really like each other. Understand?"

Ellen's forehead bunched. She didn't have any idea what Shirley was talking about, so she shook her head No.

"Think of this—someone says something; the other person says something back. Next thing you know, everybody's trying to hurt everybody else because their own feelings got hurt. Got it now?"

Ellen looked down at Shirley's sneakers, the worn white spots at the knees of Shirley's dungarees. "Whose feelings got hurt?" she asked. The horns started again.

Shirley tossed the cigarette in the street. In a voice that was gruff, but good-natured, she said, "What am I explaining to you for? Never mind. It's none of your business. This is between me and your Mom. Now, I'm riding you home. So just get your butt in that car before I tan your hide, too."

Chapter 11

THE NEXT TIME Timmy went down to Unemployment, he stood in line behind Michael Wurster. Michael's chin beard was full and thick now and he'd trimmed it to a point, which he stroked continuously as he spoke. It seemed he was in the same poetry class as Chuck Daniels. "Let me show you," Michael said, opening a 3-ring binder and removing a lined sheet of paper. The poem on it read;

> This is the dark
> This is the night
> This is the time
> Dark
> Night
> This was

"I'm thinking of calling it 'The Time'," Michael said, adjusting his red beret back up on his forehead so his right eye wasn't completely covered. "What do you think?"

Timmy shrugged. His stomach was queasy, and the muscles in his back and neck were so knotted it felt like his body was stippled with welts. Poetry, he thought. What the hell was happening to this city? He gave a quick shudder.

Michael mimicked Timmy's shudder with one of his own.

"Yeah, it made me feel that way, too. Anyways.." His voice had the chattering quality of a chipmunk's. "Theodore said it needs more images of industrial structures. But I think it's got enough. I mean, night, dark, time. When I was growing up on the South Side slopes, you could look out all the *time* at *niqht* in the *dark* and see the mills flaring orange and these big black clouds of smoke, all these reflections off the river."

Timmy nodded. He looked past the counter. Mr. King-chester's desk was empty. Jeez, was that guy on break all the time?

Michael, his voice low, agitated, stepped closer and told Timmy how his class was going to go to a real poetry reading some night. By Theodore's MFA students. MFA? Timmy wondered. Motherfuckers Anonymous? He didn't ask. He didn't want to know. Thing is, he was having trouble concentrating on what Michael was saying. It took effort just to get his feet to shuffle forward so he could hold his place in line.

The next thing he knew, Michael was holding a check aloft, giving it a dramatic kiss, and then Timmy was passing his I.D. across the counter. The woman brought it to Mr. King-chester, who'd returned from wherever he'd been. The man gave Timmy a wide, feline grin. The woman returned to the front, her lips tight, smug, and told Timmy his file was missing.

"What do you mean?" Timmy asked.

"Do I stutter? Missing. Misplaced. Maybe next time it will show up. Next." She looked around him.

Timmy pressed his fingertips so hard to the counter they turned a bruise-colored red. He breathing grew shallow and hard. Behind him, people closed in, moving forward. A man with a cigarette stuck in the corner of his mouth said, "C'mon pal. Let's move it."

"I want to talk to him." Timmy said, pointing his chin towards Mr. Kingchester. The woman looked back at her supervisor, who was still staring, smiling. As if he'd heard Timmy's request, he pursed his lips and shook his head.

"He's busy," the woman said.

Timmy raised his arms, pleading and pointing in silent exasperation. "I got people here," the woman said, her eyelids peeling so wide he could see the full roundness of her pupils.

"Hey, buddy, bad luck, but the rest of us got things to do," the man behind him said.

Timmy glanced at the line. It stretched out the door and down the sidewalk. He lowered his head and left.

Okay, hold on, he told himself. At least he could go to the food pantry. He had to take two buses, but he arrived in less than an hour. The same black woman was behind the desk. When she pulled out Timmy's file, she gave him a sympathetic look and told him he could only get a bag once a month.

"Once a month?" Timmy was incredulous. "What good is that? We got to eat every week."

"I know it's not much," she said. "I wish we could do more. But we do have a soup kitchen, you can get a hot lunch Monday through Friday, 10:30 to 12:30."

"Soup kitchen?" In his mind, Timmy pictured drunken old men in shabby coats, coughing and hacking up phlegm as they waited in line for a ladle of gruel. He was incapable of imagining himself and Pat coming in for that; holding Ellen by the hand; wheeling Katie.

"If there are special circumstances," the woman at the desk said, "you can talk to Mary."

There ain't nothing special about my circumstances, Timmy thought. But he nodded anyway.

He was led into a narrow closet of a room. The shelves on both sides were lined with canned goods and odd, balled-up pieces of clothing. The packed grocery bags took up so much of the floor space, he almost had to turn sideways to make it down the thin, winding trail to the back of the room where, beneath a leaded-glass window, at a desk covered with a chaos of paper-work, a large-boned woman, fortyish, with high, angular cheekbones and a shaved head, dropped her pencil to the desk and turned to Timmy. She put her hands on her knees and looked at him with clear-eyed attention. The muted light coming through the window softened her face, but there were deep, brown circles beneath her eyes. "Well, what's your story?" she said. She tipped some ice cubes from a paper cup into her mouth and started crunching them.

Timmy started in about his family and the lay-off and the difficulty of finding work. She cut him off by shaking her hand. She twisted around to look at his file card and asked, "Why are you back here so soon?"

He stood for a second, breathing in the sour-smelling air, the scent of it reminding him of locker rooms. Looking down at the grimed cement floor, he told her they'd lost his unemployment check.

She smiled easily, leaned back in the chair, folded her arms beneath her heavy breasts. "Okay. Take a bag."

She returned to her paperwork. Timmy stood, unmoving, waiting to be asked to justify his needs more. She looked over at him, amused, and pointed at the bags lined along the floor. "Help yourself."

He lifted a bag from the floor, feeling the urge to run out of there before this woman changed her mind. But a middle-aged black woman wearing a long black coat and a white knit hat blocked his way. She'd parked a rickety, wire-frame carriage in the doorway and was struggling to fit her full bag of groceries inside. The black woman kept looking at Timmy, scrutinizing his face. He pretended not to notice, but it was like she was trying to come to some kind of judgement about him.

"Hope that helps," Mary said to Timmy's back.

"Money would help more," he said. He felt stupid. He'd meant getting his check, but it hadn't come out that way.

"I'll pray for you," Mary told him without looking up.

Outside, on the sidewalk, the black woman turned to Timmy. "I got two boys of my own and three grandkids and they none of 'em can't walk by my refrigerator without all the time saying 'Eat, eat'." She examined Timmy's face and stood there as if waiting for something. He looked at her rheumy eyes behind her black-framed glasses, the determined set of her mouth. She peeped into his bag. "I can give you $5 for that bag. No more."

He stood on the sidewalk long after he'd settled the bag into the woman's cart and received three crumpled bills and two dollars worth of nickels and dimes in return. He was staring off, thinking about nothing, when a scraping, shuffling sound broke his reverie. He turned, looked in the direction of the fountain whose rusted people were bent backwards in agony, and was startled to see one of the figures stepping down off its stand, moving towards him. The figure stumbled in the street and Timmy realized it was just a man. A paper bag peeped from the pocket of the man's yellow corduroy jacket. Timmy skipped his eyes past the man, to the small group of other men hanging out in front of the liquor store in the block of shops behind the fountain.

"Hey," the man said, his voice thick, greasy.

Timmy shoved the money in his pocket and backed away. "I'm broke," he said.

"I seen you sell that bag."

"Bullshit," Timmy said, his eyes narrowing.

"Bullshit yourself. Give me half or I'm telling Mary."

With a sense of anger and desperation, Timmy said, "She won't believe a drunk."

The man steadied himself on a parking meter. He tried to stand straight, but started coughing and had to bend at the waist.

Timmy turned and jogged to the corner. There was nothing wrong with what he'd done, he told himself. He was helping out a woman who needed it. She had a family to take care of; he had a family to take care of. The bus was just pulling in, a big poster on its side of a blonde woman and a dark-haired man, MIKE AND EDIE ARE ON THIS BUS. Timmy ran and vaulted up the steps, then worked his way towards the rear. As he sat on a hard, plastic seat it came to him; what the hell good was $5? It would take three times that to buy a bag of groceries. What was he thinking? That money was it? Money was what he needed? Money itself, and not the things it could buy? Here he was thinking and worrying so much about not having any money, and what had he done? What was happening to him? He thought of the transaction with the woman at the massage parlor, this transaction here. What the hell kind of man was he anymore? What had he become? What right did he have to show his face at his home? What right did he even have to call it home?

When the bus halted, he turned from the hill, instead went down where the street gullied, cut under the railroad overpass. He headed for Harry's. At least I'm not like that man with the bottle in his pocket, he told himself. At least I can still afford to sit in a bar and drink. But the bulge of change in his pocket made him uneasy. In his mind there arose the question, Yeah, but for how long?

He paused outside Harry's door and clenched his hands. Please God, let Jim be here, he thought. Let him show up. I need somebody to talk to. But the scene inside made him forget, temporarily, his concerns.

The place was mobbed. "What gives?" Timmy asked, settling on a stool near the front. Harry flicked his cloth over the bar in a pretense of wiping. "Your buddy must've hit the lottery. When someone's buying, it don't take two minutes for word to get out."

Timmy looked down the length of the bar and spotted Gerry, making his way up towards him. Gerry, his face florid and smiling, received handshakes, pats on his arms and chest, as he headed to the front.

"Here he is!" Gerry said, gripping Timmy around the shoulders and nearly pulling him off the stool. "Steelers! Steelers!" he chanted, then laughed to the room. "On me," Gerry told Harry. He pulled a wad of twenties from his pocket. Harry waved him off. "I'll let you know when I use up what you already gave me."

"You," Gerry said as Timmy accepted a shot and a beer. Gerry punched him in the arm. "If I hadn't bounced your car back from that hydrant, you'd have about a thousand bucks in tickets right now."

The man to Timmy's right said, "They got no business

ticketing a man's car." Timmy and Gerry looked over. The man had a body like a cement mixer gone soft. His face was dark and lumpy, scarred around the eyes. His nose had been broken at least twice. He spoke in an angry ramble. "Problem is, everyone's in your business, but if someone's giving you the business, that's none of your business."

Gerry gave Timmy an amused look, then leaned over. "Yeah, buddy. Have another drink. Harry!" He raised his arm and motioned at the man with his finger. Harry came over and put his hands to the wooden counter. "Cheer this son of a bitch up," Gerry said. "I'm going to go play some records."

Timmy looked around. Jim wasn't there. Timmy didn't want to feel ungrateful towards Gerry, but beyond the Steelers, the arm punching and laughter, they had nothing between them.

The man beside him knocked his elbow into Timmy's arm. "Whatever happened to Big Business?" the man said.

"I don't know," Timmy said and lifted his beer.

The man hit Timmy's arm again. "A few years back, everyone was complaining 'Big Business this', 'Big Business that'. Now that so many more things are screwed up, how come nobody wants to blame Big Business? Somebody's got to be at fault."

Harry stared at the man. "Bad? Don't you watch the news? We're going through a friggin' Renaissance. We're the number one city in the country. Things are friggin' great."

"What things?" the man asked, pushing back in his seat belligerently.

Timmy glanced around for Gerry. This guy made him nervous. He acted like one of those guys who kept talking until they got so pissed off they had to hit somebody.

"What things?" Harry repeated, straightening up and adjusting the wash cloth tucked into the tie strap of his apron. "If you listen to the news, every-friggin'-thing is going smooth as baby shit. Don't you never listen to our beloved mayor?"

Laughter cracked along the bar like falling dominos as Harry walked off. The guy beside Timmy waved his hand and said, "That little fuckin' wop."

"He died," Timmy said, shaking his head.

The guy looked at him. "The wop?"

"Yeah." Timmy spoke out the side of his mouth without turning. "A while ago. We got a new mayor. An old Jewish lady. She's about 70 years old or something."

"A Jew?" The guy looked around, as if seeking an audience. "First we had to let the niggers in the mill, then we had to let women. Now you got women and nigger cops, firemen, everything you can imagine."

"Come on," someone said down the bar. Harry looked over, his jaw gone rigid.

"You come on," the guy said. "They're giving jobs to fucking homos and Japs—everybody but us white guys. And now you're telling me there's a kike running the city?" His eyelids opened so wide it seemed he was offering his eyeballs for the plucking. "How come everybody gets a break but us? Huh?" He turned on his stool and opened his hands to the room.

"That's enough of that," Harry said.

"Enough of what?" The man pushed his stool back from the bar.

There were a few muttered sounds of embarrassment, but mostly everyone remained silent. Timmy glanced around. The people in the place looked the same as usual—dungarees and workshirts, guys holding their beer bottles at their sides, like they were clubs—but few of their faces were familiar. Who the hell are these guys? he wondered. Where did they come from? Where did they work? He looked closely at their faces. The men had glazed eyes, with folds of skin under them like hardened dough. Their mouths seemed set into frowns, like they couldn't smile if they wanted to. There was a sucked-in look to their cheeks, like they'd been in a pressure chamber. Their skin seemed drained of all fluid.

He turned back to the bar, drank from his mug. He listened to the commercials on the TV, the tapping, scraping sound of bottles and glasses on wood. He stared at his own image in the mirror above the bottles behind the bar and realized, he looked just as bad as everyone else in here.

"Well come on. Tell me. Enough of what?" The man stood. He was about 6'3", 250 pounds. He shook his arms loose.

"The Boss," Gerry said, giving Timmy's shoulders a squeeze as he came back. He motioned for another round.

The sound exploded through the bar, drums and power chords, and Gerry was jumping up, bouncing strumming an imaginary guitar, punching his fist in the air as he sung along to Bruce Springsteen's "Born in the USA."

"That's what I'm talking about," the guy beside Timmy screamed. The man's face was on the brittle edge of anger. No one would look at him now, except Gerry.

"What's your problem buddy?" Gerry said.

The man's body went taut, his gaze fixed on the mirror. A minor trembling passed through him like a sparking current.

Hands gripped Timmy's shoulders and gave them a squeeze. "Hey, you munchkin," someone said, and Timmy turned to see Jim's smiling face.

Springsteen's gravelly shout cut through the bar, singing about having nowhere to run, nowhere to go.

Timmy saw it coming out the side of his eye, but it went so quickly he had no time to warn Jim. In one motion the man swiped a beer bottle from the bar and smashed it into Jim's face. The bottle exploded on impact. As Gerry and several others jumped on the man, knocking him to the floor, Timmy watched Jim stagger back, a jagged river of blood as wide as a finger flowed from a gash above Jim's left eye. Jim's knees bent, his feet did a desperate zig-zag dance as he struggled to remain standing. Then his legs collapsed on him. Timmy leaped from his stool and grabbed Jim's arm, pulling on it hard enough to break Jim's fall.

Gerry and three guys kicked and punched the other man as they pushed him towards the door. That man kept trying to rise, getting to his hands and knees, but workboots pounded his ribs until he fell again. Timmy watched until the man was shoved out onto the sidewalk, and Gerry returned, brushing his hands. Harry had already called 911.

FAITH IN WHAT?

They propped Jim into a sitting position against the bar and pressed a clean white cloth against his wound. "I didn't know you hated the name Munchkin so much," he joked, but Timmy couldn't laugh. He felt it was somehow his fault, what had happened, and he didn't know what to say. He couldn't even make the small amend of driving Jim to the hospital, because Timmy didn't have a car to drive. One of the guys came over, who had some training in first aid, and Timmy stepped back to let that man do what he could for Jim. Then the ambulance people were there, insisting, above Jim's protests, that he had to go in for stitches, and the wound was bleeding too heavily for him to drive himself. Timmy thought of offering to drive Jim's car, but the medics were already moving Jim to the door.

Timmy leaned his elbows onto the worn counter. He looked at the way the overhead fluorescent bar lights gleamed on the bottles lined in three staggered rows on the shelves before him. He remembered how the bottles had seemed to glitter, back when he'd been working, as if the fingers of light were flames, beckoning him to celebrate, promising Timmy there were secrets inside those bottles, the contained depths and nuances that went into making a person. Drinking, sampling his way from bottle to bottle through an evening's drunk, Timmy would feel energized, like he was doing something good, figuring out something about himself, and the people around him.

Now, though, the light looked trapped, like bubbles caught in the quick ice of a puddle. The bottles seemed insubstantial, thin. He knew if he broke them all open he'd find nothing—just a space of air, a bit of liquid, all of it adding up to —What?

Gerry patted Timmy's shoulders. "Hey buddy, cheer up. He'll be okay."

Timmy shook his head. "I went through this whole day, and I didn't do nothing that mattered to anyone."

"Yeah, sure," Gerry said nodding, combing his fingers through his beard.

They sat drinking quietly through the rest of the

afternoon. When the news came on, the guys left in the bar turned their attention to that. The lead story was about the Hardhat Bandit. He'd hit another bank. Gerry pulled his stool tight to the bar and listened intently. Sandy Cooper, tipping her head this way and that, as if she were examining the small shiny spot on her nose in a mirror, said the mayor was forming a special task force to capture the bandit. "Hey, it's a posse," Harry said, and most of the guys at the bar smiled. Then Mayor Stephanie Mendelson's long, rectangular face came on the screen. A thick sedge of red hair sat atop her wide, high forehead. In the glare from the TV camera's light, her skin had the orange waxy tone of a cadaver. She spoke in a shrill voice, her teeth showing yellow. "This is a city of decent, honest working people. That penny-ante deadbeat must be from New York." Her mouth closed like a puppet's.

Gerry's face had darkened in anger. "What does she know?" he said. "She never sweated a day in her life." He drank from his mug.

On the jukebox, a woman sang in a tremulous voice that people were talking about making a revolution.

"See?" Gerry said. He nodded back at the jukebox. Timmy listened. The song seemed to float through the bar like a flashlight beam, searching for something to illuminate. The women sang about poor people rising up, getting their share. Timmy looked around the bar. Everyone seemed to be slumped in their chairs. Is that what we've become? Is that what I am? A poor person? He listened to the chorus, the word 'run' repeating over and over, and he felt afraid.

"What am I gonna do?" He tipped the shot glass to his mouth and felt the burn along the inside of his throat.

"Problem with these guys," Gerry said, "is someone did all their thinking for them all their lives. Their daddies, the union, the foremen. Now there's no one to take care of them anymore. They're being asked to use their brains, and they don't know how. They're out of practice. "

Timmy ran his fingers through a circle of moisture on the bar. "Didn't you used to have faith?" Timmy asked. "I used to believe there'd be jobs for guys who wanted to work; the unions would look out for your ass; this city cared. I thought my family..." His voice choked and he was stunned. Quickly, he scooped up a cocktail napkin and pretended to sneeze, so he could wipe his eyes.

"What about your family?" Gerry said, his hand growing hot on Timmy's back. "You having trouble with them buddy?"

"Them?" Timmy made a small, scoffing sound. He turned to Gerry, whose hard eyes were as depthless as a cat's. "I got nothing to believe in anymore. Nothing. What's ever gonna get better? You know, I used to be a pretty good husband and father. I was a good provider." He squeezed his fists.

Gerry stroked his beard with one hand and patted Timmy's shoulder with the other. He appeared to be deliberating. Cutting his eyes along the length of the bar to be sure no one was listening, he leaned close. "You want to do something make you feel like a man again?"

"I'm not talking about getting laid," Timmy said, turning impatiently.

Gerry pulled him back around. "I'm not either," he said. "I'm talking about something big, something wilder than anything even I ever thought of before. Something to shake everyone up. Make 'em really pay attention to what's happening to this city."

Timmy looked at him closely. "What?"

Gerry smiled. "Something to blow the mayor's mind."

Chapter 12

I PICKED UP the flyers from the copy shop in our little downtown section. The guy who worked there during the day, his name was Hank. He used to be at the Homestead plant before they let him go. He's one of these guys who's got a heart as big as the world if he knows you, but he hates everyone he don't know—Blacks, Japanese, Arabs, womens' righters, homos. It's embarrassing, because he always assumes you hate those people, too. But he's been good to me; always makes me free copies when his boss ain't around. Gave me some Debbie's cakes to bring home to the kids for Halloween. What, am I supposed to not let him be nice to me? It amazes me sometimes when I think about the people I've had to rely on. People I never in a million years would've had anything to do with if this hadn't happened in my life.

I looked at the picture of Katie on the flyer as I walked up the hill to the church. I wasn't used to walking and my knee was killing me. "See what I put myself through for you," I said to her picture, stopping to rub my knee. When I bent over, my back muscles pulled tight, and I had to straighten up really slow. Our car was still parked down to Gerry's, where Timmy had left it. We didn't even have the money to tow it somewhere to see what needed fixed. I felt like I should be angry at someone for that. But who?

FAITH IN WHAT?

A breeze snapped past and I had to clutch the flyers tight so they wouldn't get blown away. Katie's face seemed to smile right at me. Only it didn't look like Katie's face anymore. It wasn't just my bad drawing, either. She was so much older now, her face so different, but not in a good way. Not like you see kids get older and you notice, especially in their eyes, that they know more and —I don't know how to explain this—it's like, they know things can hurt them, but they also know there are more things to be excited about than just toys. I guess it's they're learning about hope and fear, and trying to figure out how to keep the hope, and not let the fear take over.

Katie's face in the drawing had hope in it, the way any little kid's face from a normal home does: that little kid hope about good things happening, having fun, being happy. When I thought of what she looked like now—her face had nothing in it. I'd give anything to see her look like a six-year-old again. A two-year-old. To for Christ's sake even crawl like a baby.

Our church has long, wide stone steps leading up to a big, open foyer where we have coffee and pastries set up on folding tables the second Sunday of every month. That was coming up this week. It's called Share Sunday. People are supposed to get together and socialize. Mostly, though, they hang around for the free food. I figured this was as good a time as any to leave flyers at the church.

The magazine rack is by the door, beside the marble basin full of holy water. I tucked some "Katie's Gonna Win" flyers between the copies of "Our Sunday Visitor," and a slick brochure explaining why missionaries working in some foreign country needed my donation. Take care of your own first, I thought. Then I dipped my hand into the holy water and blessed myself; in the name of the Father, Son, and the Holy Ghost. I rubbed the water across my eyes, praying, Lord help me see clearly; I poked a wet finger in each ear, praying, Lord help me to listen; I ran my fingers down my tongue, praying, Lord, help me to speak. After that, I dipped my hand in the water again, then rubbed it on my knee and my back. Making sure nobody was coming in from outside, I filled an old sippy cup with water, snapped on the top, and put it in my bag to take home to Katie. Then I went in to confession.

There were half a dozen old ladies already in the church. I could tell by the way they snapped their heads back to the front altar, that they'd all been watching me—the foyer is separated from the church by a wall of glass. Get a good look? I felt like saying. I knelt near the back, thinking, God, I can't even come in here without getting angry. I wondered if He was going to hold that against Katie, too. Isn't that the way it worked? The kids had to pay for the sins of the parents? I lifted my head from my folded hands and looked at the altar.

We have a new Christ in our church. There used to be one of those life-sized plaster models of Jesus bleeding on the cross, the crown of thorns stuck into His head, the hole in His side weeping blood as thick and red as ketchup. But our pastor, Father Hogg, had replaced that with a statue of a risen Christ who floated over the altar, His hands parted as if asking us to rise. Two small rainbows curved on either side of Him, and He wore a robe which covered His skin from His neck to his feet. In a way, I liked the other one better, although this one was easier to take. I could make a real confession with the old Christ nailed there. This new Christ, I don't know. He was too lovey-dovey or something. He looked like a pushover. It was like I could put things past Him; even if He caught on, he'd be too nice to say anything.

I knelt with my butt catching the lip of the pew, trying to remember the words of confession. Bless me Father for I have sinned, my last confession was...when? And these are my sins. I thought for a long time. Three of the black-veiled women entered the confessional, and the first two were now kneeling at the altar as they prayed their penance. I couldn't remember what I'd just been thinking about. It was like I'd been brain dead for fifteen minutes. I felt a flicker of fear go through my heart, because both my mother and father had died from strokes, and just before their big ones, they started getting forgetful. Then, too, Katie.

FAITH IN WHAT?

I concentrated hard. Confession, I thought. Bless me Father. Sins. Could I just say I was disobedient? Wouldn't that cover everything? Every sin was a disobedience of one sort or another, wasn't it? I looked up at the Christ and thought, Let's cut the crap, You know why I'm here. I don't care about my sins. I need You to fix my little girl.

I sat in the pew to wait my turn with the priest. I thought about this God, sending His son down to be crucified on a cross. How could You do that? I wondered. How could You love everybody else so much that You would let Your own kid die—and not just die, but put Him through this humiliation and torture? It's a good thing You picked Mary and not me to be Jesus' mother, I thought, because I wouldn't have put up with it. I would've taken someone's Goddamned sword and sliced off more than a few ears. There would've been two of us up on crosses and I would've been yelling, for everyone to hear, What the Hell You think You're doing? Then I realized how stupid that was; like I'm a candidate to be the mother of God.

In my head, it was almost like He was talking to me, only I think it was just myself, talking back in His voice, pointing out that every child is God's child, so in a way I was the mother of God. Or at least a little piece of Him. Well then, I argued, what are you doing with Katie? Aren't you just torturing yourself?

But if she was paying for my sins, I thought, if God was taking it out on her for some way I screwed up...Well then, You're a prick, I told Him. If You want to do something to me, do it to me. Don't make my baby suffer if I'm the asshole.

It was the most incredible thing then. It wasn't like I heard anything, or saw anything. But I got this feeling, sort of like a vibration going on inside me. I swore, if I just sat there and waited, something would be made clear to me. But I got scared. First, I didn't know what it was. I mean, of course I thought it was Him. But I didn't *know*. Then I thought, what if what He said made sense? What if he was trying to explain to me about Katie's illness. What if it was meant to be? I got so scared I almost wet my pants. I didn't want to hear it. I wanted change, not an explanation. I shook my head so hard, saying to myself, Don't give me no excuses; I won't listen; I just want You to make my Katie normal again.

That's when Father Hogg came out. I figured one of the old ladies must've told him, because he stepped from the confessional and began shaking his finger as he walked towards me down the aisle. At the rail around the altar, one of the women turned and I could see the smug set of her mouth. Bless you too, I thought.

Father Hogg is a heavy, bald-headed, square-faced man who wears those old, thick-framed glasses. As he stopped beside me, his mouth hung open like a large puncture, the type of hole an axe might make in a cardboard box. "I've warned you before..." he started in.

"I'm not asking for money, just help."

"If we do it for one, we've got to do it for everyone." He stood in the aisle, looking down at me where I sat.

"What's wrong with that? Isn't that what a church is supposed to do?"

His mouth closed like a turtle's, clean, tight, and lipless. He pushed his glasses up with his thumb. Behind the lenses, his gray, tired-looking eyes were as small and hard as bullets. "Remove them, or I'll personally throw them in the rubbish," he said.

I shuffled out of the pew. "Yeah, the Lord be with you, too," I said, looking down at where his black robe swayed over his expensive wing-tip cordovans.

Behind me, the glass door gave a small squeak. I glanced back and saw Shirley. That made me tense up even more. "What's going on here?" she asked.

Father Hogg made a brushing motion with his hand without looking at her. "We'll pray for you," he told me dismissively.

"Pray for yourself," I said. "How many times have you been to my house to help?" I quickly turned and headed down the aisle.

Behind me, he rattled off his spiel about the time-consuming responsibilities of a priest. I knew: cake sales, fund raisers, book discussion groups. Bingo. As I walked, I thought of how this was the same aisle I'd traveled, only in the other direction, the day I was married. For better or worse. Why didn't the church make that same commitment?

I went into the foyer and snatched up the flyers. Shirley was still standing in the aisle, watching. I meant to shake the flyers at Father Hogg, but something—I don't know what—took hold of me. Maybe it was Shirley being there, giving me that look like, don't take any crap from this guy. I stormed back into the church and threw the stack up as high as I could. They scattered apart, fluttered down among the pews; Katie's smiling face falling all around me. "You look at her for a change," I said, knowing, as I spoke, I was saying it half for Shirley's benefit. "You look at her and then go ahead and throw her out yourself," I told him. "*Mister* Hogg."

"Hey," Shirley said. She grabbed up a flyer and held it out to him. With her other hand, she tugged on the sleeve of his robe. He looked stunned that she had touched him. "Last Sunday you let this nun come in, college-educated broad wearing a pants suit half the people in this church could never afford to buy. She gives us this guilt trip about how we owe her so she can retire, take things easy."

Shirley glanced over, gave me a secret wink. I watched her cautiously. Father Hogg was upset—you could tell by the moustache of sweat above his top lip. Shirley turned back to him. "I don't remember Jesus saying, Hey hold off on that Sermon on the Mount, I got vacation time coming. Moses didn't tell the Jews, Okay, now that I got the ten commandments for you, you owe me a condo in Florida. You see what I'm saying? Either you're working for God, or you ain't. What's this retirement crap? And what's this that we got to pay for it? We're fucking working people."

"Watch your language in the house of the Lord," Father Hogg managed.

It was like she was a pitcher for the Pirates, the way Shirley pulled her hand back and threw her pointing finger forward at him. "Watch your work," she said.

I was as shocked as Father Hogg. We both stood there as Shirley scooped up a handful of flyers. "This is the point I'm making. Pat's been coming to this church since before you even heard of Pittsburgh. It's more her church than yours for Christ's sake—and I do mean for Christ's sake. If you're gonna let them other jokers hit on us for money, least you can do is let Pat ask for help," she said.

"Everything has to be approved by the diocese," Father Hogg said tiredly.

"Diocese my ass," Shirley told him.

She walked to the side wall, where the carved metal plaques depicting the Stations of the Cross began. "You got any tape?" she said. When no one answered, she shrugged her shoulders and stuffed a flyer behind the first station, angling it sideways so that you could read it. She walked towards the front of the church, tucking a flyer behind each plaque, until Katie's smiling face accompanied Jesus on every step of His walk to Calvary.

We sat in the type of bar that used to serve us back when we were under age. It was real narrow, a single strip of space lit by yellow bulbs glaring from bare sockets. The bulbs were so old and dust-covered you could look at them all day and they wouldn't hurt your eyes. The air was as stiff as cardboard, with a smell kind of like old baby diarrhea. We knew there'd only be a few people in the place, and that's all there were. Four men, wearing flannel shirts, feed caps on their heads, sitting on stools. Me and Shirley had been sitting in one of the booths for God knows how long, drinking up a storm. "Two more root beers for Chrissakes," she called to the bartender, making the sign of the cross to the room as if blessing it. I laughed so hard my sides hurt. She was laughing, too, one of those loud, screeching type laughs. We'd been laughing since we'd come in the place, and, at first, everyone else got a kick out of it. It made them laugh, too. But by now, you could tell, it got on their nerves, because they didn't have nothing to really laugh about.

"Fuck 'em," Shirley said, "They don't like it."

"Well if we're gonna fuck 'em, we have to divvie them up," I said, and she howled.

"Do you want the guy who looks like someone took a bite out of his nose?" I asked. I nodded at a white-haired guy who had one of those big Polish noses that looked like people had gouged chunks out of with a screwdriver.

"Ain't you the one always liked a smooth talker?" she said, motioning at the man sitting on the stool at the rear of the bar. His face was to the wood and he was muttering what sounded like a list of all the swear words he could think of.

I laughed so hard I had to start making hooting sounds, to get myself to stop. But that only started Shirley in laughing harder, which made me laugh harder.

"Oh God," I said. "I feel like I lost twenty pounds."

"Probably did," Shirley said, "paying for this crap." The bartender brought over two more shot glasses full of root beer schnapps. She hefted her shot, crossed her eyes, and downed half, grimacing when she was finished. I had a mouthful of schnapps and, seeing her, I laughed and spit it out all over the table. "Dress you up, but can't take you anywhere," Shirley said. She jerked a wad of napkins from the dispenser and dabbed at her sweater—a plain brown acrylic one with a small vee neck—then at the tabletop.

"Big Daddy on the mound," I said. "Here's the wind-up." I pulled my arm back and pitched my finger at her. "Watch your work," we yelled together, and then we both screamed.

I felt so relaxed, unburdened. "We should do this more often," I said.

"What's wrong with once every six years?"

I started to laugh, then stopped. "Six years?"

"Think about it," Shirley said, lighting a cigarette. She

blew a funnel of smoke up towards the ceiling. "This is the first time we been out together since, what? Katie been sick? I'm not talking visiting across the street. I mean out, out."

"No, it can't be." I put my hands to the surface of the booth. The wood was worn and had that gummy feel. There were initials and hearts and arrows gouged into the table, claims of love for eternity, one crude drawing of a large-breasted woman over by the napkin dispenser. When I thought of what Shirley had just said, I knew she was right. I didn't want to believe it. I even felt my head giving a shake, as if trying to deny it. But I hadn't gone anywhere with friends since this whole thing started. And other than running errands, or a few times sitting on the porch, I hadn't gone anywhere alone. And Ellen and Timmy—when had I last done anything fun with either of them? "I miss the outside world," I said.

Shirley tapped the ash from her cigarette into the silver cardboard ashtray. She ran the cone-shaped ember along the edge of it.

"I mean, I don't regret, we made this decision together. Katie's our kid, and this is what we're going to do. I mean, family is family, and I'm not saying I regret making this decision. I wish none of it had happened, but it did, so what choice did we really have? But still I, you know, I miss...it"

"At least you and Timmy must get out sometimes, right?"

I had to shake my head. "Who's going to take care of Katie? We can't leave her with a sitter. What if she has a seizure?"

"How about your in-laws?"

I gave her a look. "They're in Florida."

"Yeah, I forgot."

"They can't handle it anyways. I swear that's what finally decided them to retire down there."

"Come on, you don't believe that." Shirley finished her shot. "They were talking about moving when I first knew you. "

I had to admit it. But admitting it, I felt deprived. It was like I wanted to believe they'd run out on us; like I wanted an excuse to feel sorry for myself or something.

"You gotta do something," Shirley said. "You'll go nuts if *you* at least don't get out. I know Jim, Christ, he drives me crazy. He's such a puppy. When I'm home, he follows me around from room to room, telling me everything he heard on TV, or read about. I says to him one day, Why don't you just cut out the newspaper and glue it onto your eyeballs, then you can read it direct?"

I laughed, but it was one of those sad laughs. Shirley nodded.

"I know it ain't his fault." She dragged on her cigarette again, twirled it between her fingers. "No one expected everything to fall apart just when our guys were starting to get their lives set up." Her eyes went over my face, then she sort of twisted her mouth sideways to exhale against the wall. "These guys though, you know? They're sooo lost." She touched my hand with hers and leaned closer, cutting her eyes sideways to see if we were being watched. I could feel myself shaking, I wanted to take my hand away so bad, but I was more afraid if I did that she'd leave. "Give 'em a job, and they've got a cock two feet long," Shirley said. "But when they're laid off, shit, you gotta wipe their nose and ass for them. They're like six foot tall toddlers, yapping at you 'Mommy mommy mommy.'"

She drew on her cigarette, tasted the smoke, let it dribble out her nose as she looked down at the table. "I get so sick and tired of having to hold the house together, go out and get extra work myself, treat my husband with kid gloves—I got to suck Jim off for half an hour, my mouth's so goddamned tired I can hardly talk—me, right?—just to get him hard enough so I can get laid." She opened her hands and eyes, assuming I would agree with her. I nodded as if I did, as if I still touched Timmy, as if I could even remember the last time we did anything like that together.

Shirley looked at me closely, then sat back in the booth. "It's not that I resent it. Well, of course, I mean, you resent it. But it's, he's my husband, he's going through a tough time."

I started to think of Timmy, hanging around all morning

in his pajamas, trying to smile, only not really being able to. It was like the muscles of his face were frozen into a frown, or the flesh around his jaw was so heavy, his lips couldn't curve up. I thought of him lying in bed at night, waiting for me—I knew, because I always saw the light on when I brushed my teeth before heading back down to the couch.

Shirley lit another cigarette from the butt of her old one. "But hell, so am I, and I don't see nobody giving a shit about that. You hear all this crap about workers this, workers that. What about us? Me and the kids? You. All the other women and kids. We're in this mess, too." She touched her chest with her hand. "This ain't no joyride, the shit we gotta go through. I mean, you marry this big, strong guy with arms like Popeye...but then you find out, these guys are so *fragile*. It's like they're made out of glass. Anything goes wrong, and they just shatter. And they don't know shit about what to do next. I feel like one day I was standing there, taking care of my family, minding my own business. The next day, someone piled a load of bricks on my back. Every day since Jim got laid off, someone's been piling more and more bricks on me, and there ain't no sign it's gonna stop."

We were silent for a while. The bartender came over with the bottle of schnapps and we both nodded for him to fill us up. "Ah, it could be worse," Shirley said, then took a sip. "I mean, you see all the women coming in to church with black eyes, broken lips. I heard, Maureen McCarthy told me, about this one guy she knows, sold his son's bike and football and everything, just so's he could go drinking."

I knew these things were supposed to make me feel better. Shirley knew it, too. But she looked at me and I looked back and we both knew—the trouble in other people's lives didn't matter. We had our own problems to deal with. Knowing things were worse for someone else didn't change our own situations.

"You been awful quiet," she said. She pointed the two fingers holding her cigarette at my face. "You got that look, like I'm talking Greek. What's the matter? What's going on?"

"Sometimes I try," I told her, wondering if this were the

truth, the real truth, or if it was just something I wanted to believe about myself. "I try to be in a good mood for Timmy, but then he does something so stupid, or he says something, and I get so pissed off. It's like, when I'm home, I'm looking for reasons to be angry at him, or, or waiting for him to do something so I can be pissed off. Then when he does something, it's like, 'Ah-ha!'. I knew you'd do something. I feel justified."

She gave me a little smirk. "I went through that."

"You did?"

She nodded, dragging on her cigarette. "Yeah. I was feeling like all this crap that happened was somehow my fault. Like I was being blamed for it. So I tried to get back at everyone. You know? Find all kinds of little things to blame them for. I made Jim and Jimmy Junior miserable. Finally I figured out those guys were just as freaked out by this whole thing as I was." She looked at me and shrugged her eyebrows. "It wasn't none of our faults. None of us asked to get screwed over. But we'd been made to feel like somehow we were responsible. You know? We just started attacking each other.

"So one day I says to myself, Shirley, this is stupid. Think about who your real enemy is here. You know? It's like, whoever is responsible for screwing up our lives set us against each other so we'd be too busy fighting each other to see who was really responsible."

I was watching her face as she spoke. She was a hard-looking woman, no doubt about it. But her eyes now seemed to soften, take on the look of a teenager who has just been dumped for the first time. They were full of a new, painful understanding, an awareness that things she had no control over could hurt her. "Well who is responsible?" I asked her.

She tipped her head one way, then the other, twirled the cigarette in her fingers. "That's just it. You can't tell anymore. It's not like when our parents were growing up. Now, the people pulling the strings are invisible. The only ones you can see are the victims. And when you don't have nobody else to blame..."

We sat in silence for a few more moments. Then Shirley

perked up and looked around quickly. She slapped her hands on the table and rolled her eyes. "Here I am looking for a clock and I got a watch on." We had one good laugh as she checked the time. "I gotta go," she said, searching through her pocketbook for money. She tossed a few bills in a pile on the table. "You need a ride, or are you still taping those up?" She motioned to my pocketbook, the flyers sticking out.

I felt a twinge in my knee. But guilt was so deep in me, I told her, "Yeah, I'm not finished yet."

Outside, it was already dark, the streetlights on. A cold wind snapped around the corners of the buildings. I pulled my coat tight, wishing I'd remembered to sew back on the button that was missing at the top.

"Okay," Shirley said, opening the door to her car. "Give me a call if you want to swap." She had a cigarette in her mouth and she looked tough, standing there, adjusting her kerchief. I'd always admired that about her, the way she looked.

"Swap?" I said.

She took the cigarette out and pointed at me with the hand holding it. "Yeah, you can ring Jim's chimes some night while I clean Timmy's pipes." I must've had a real shocked look on my face because she said, "Gullible McGillicutty, I'm talking about the kids. You watch my kid some day, and I'll watch yours the next. That way we don't have to pay for no sitter."

I didn't know what to say, I was so surprised. She started to duck into the car then stood back up, gave me a wink. "Or maybe we'll let the guys watch 'em while we go out and pick up some young studs who are looking for broads who been around and know when to yank and when to pull."

She left me standing there, laughing, as she drove off down the street. I watched her red taillights disappear around a corner two blocks away. All up and down the street, the only lights on were streetlights, their reflections like wide, furry stripes on the road. The businesses were all closed, shut for the night. It made no sense to tape the flyers on the outsides of the window glass, because kids would only rip them down. "You jerk," I told myself; don't even pay attention to what's around you. Here I was, telling myself I was a bad person if I went back home, when the truth was, there was nothing more I could do out here tonight. All I had to show for my guilt was a long, miserable walk in the cold.

Chapter 13

"DADDY, what are you doing?" Ellen said.

Even though it was morning, and he'd only been up a few hours, Timmy felt dazed. He looked around to orient himself. He was sitting on the couch, facing the TV. Katie was in her wheelchair, to his left. Ellen, hands on her hips, her skirt twirling as she twisted back and forth, stood in the doorway to the dining room. There was a sensation of deep loss reverberating inside him, though loss for what, he couldn't say. Without thinking, he rose, crossed to the kitchen table, and pulled out a chair. Ellen turned as he passed. She was staring, smiling, still twirling her skirt. "What are you talking about?" he asked her as he sat down. He ran his hands over the white plastic tablecloth and felt his throat thicken.

"That's what I'm talking about," Ellen said, pointing at him.

Timmy looked at her without speaking.

A flicker of concern flashed across her eyes.

In the den, Katie gave out a low moan. she was hunched over, her face almost in her lap.

Timmy hurried across the room to sit her up straight. The stench of shit surrounded her like a cloud. The idea of changing her made him nauseous. Where was Pat? She'd only gone out to put up flyers, a chore that filled Timmy with such unspecified dread, he couldn't do it. He could never figure out where Pat found the strength to do all this stuff, to keep facing the reality of what Katie had become. Timmy had to practically deny her very existence to be able to function well enough to make it through each day. Every time he thought about her, he wanted to crawl off into the woods and die. It almost made him thankful for his own problems, which were so consuming he felt he was lucky to be able to think at all.

"Nobody ever cares about me. I'm going to run away."

He snapped around to her. "No!" he yelled. He lunged towards her, knowing, even as he moved, that his reaction was extreme and ridiculous. She was too surprised to do more than take a step backwards as he stooped and wrapped her in his arms. She said to him in a voice at once pleased and embarrassed, "Daddy!"

He loosened his hold, ran his hands down her arms. Already, dark hairs sprouted on her forearms. That made him sad. He knew what she'd be facing in a few years, the taunts from her classmates for being a hairy-armed girl. It pained him to realize he'd be unable to do anything to protect her from that. He couldn't provide for his kids, he couldn't protect them...wasn't there anything he could do? Was Gerry's crazy idea the only option left? He took up Ellen's hands and stroked the backs of her fingers with his thumbs. "Always remember Daddy loves you," he said.

Ellen pulled her hands free. She gave him a smile as if to say he was being silly. A gap showed where one of her front teeth had fallen out. When did that happen? he wondered. How could he not have noticed? "Daddy," she said, "you didn't answer my question."

"What question?"

Her lips vibrated as she blew out a breath. "First," she said, pulling her chin to her chest and looking out the tops of her eyes, "you sat at the table." She pointed to the far end of the kitchen table. "In that chair. Then...you sat in the next chair.

125

Then... you sat on this end of the couch. Then... in the big chair. Then... on the other end of the couch. Now you went and sat in the other kitchen chair." He followed her pointing finger around the apartment as if it were a tour guide, directing his attention. "Why did you do that,Daddy?"

He knelt on one knee, looking at her hands, the short fingernails rimmed with dirt, the smooth skin between the joints. He had no memory of moving around like that. Why *had* he done it? "Daddy's got a lot on his mind," Timmy said. Gerry's gruff voice seemed to echo in his memory; "Hey buddy, it's fourth down. You ain't gone nowhere by running straight into the line. It's time for a little razzle dazzle."

"What things?" Ellen stepped closer, her nose almost touching his. Her face held a look of such openness he thought she'd believe anything. He didn't know if he should feel grateful or mortified by that. "I think you're going cuck-oo," she said.

"You know what I think?" He put his hands around the waist of her pink T-shirt, remembering the thrill he got, when she was a baby, when he did this and his fingers touched. He stood and lifted and swung her to the couch, saying, "I think it's time for the tickle bug." She squirmed and screamed and laughed beneath his active fingers.

"I'm home," Pat called as she banged the door open. Gray light flowed in behind her.

"Mumma," Ellen said, rolling from the couch and running to Pat, who bent as if to give her a kiss, but pulled back at the last moment. Ellen pretended not to notice and clung to her mother's side. "Did you get something for me?" Ellen asked.

"You skootch! What did I go out to do?"

"Put up flyers?"

"Bingo. I didn't get nothing for nobody."

Ellen let go and started to move towards the couch. Pat halted her by saying, "But..."

Ellen twirled back, her look excited, anticipatory.

"I saw Lynn Emmanuel pushing her twins in the carriage," Pat said. Se looked up at Timmy. "Remember her? She was going to Pitt until she got pregnant and they cut off her money? Her husband had that shop, used to make raviolis shaped like monkies or apes or something?"

Timmy nodded, vaguely recalling a homemade pasta shop that opened and closed in a matter of months.

"Welllll," Pat said, turning back to Ellen. "She wondered if I knew anyone who would like this." Pat pulled forth a green lollipop shaped like a gorilla.

Ellen jumped up and down yelling "Me me me," until Pat gave it to her.

To Timmy, Pat said, "They're in the candy business now. They got cards printed up—Apes About Sugar. Get this, they only make three kinds of lollipops, green gorillas, orange orangutangs, and mauve monkies."

"Mauve?"

"Purple." Pat shook her head, then a wistful expression caused her cheeks to blush. "The twins were so cute, though." She stared at Katie and it looked like her eyes were about to water. "There's my baby." She moved over to cup Katie's chin and kiss her hair. Crinkling her nose, she added, "Pee-you, you stink." She straightened up and looked at Timmy. "Why didn't you change her?" She was still smiling, but Timmy could see her humor drain away.

Timmy said, "I was gonna, but..."

She gave a look around the apartment, as if the room itself were sucking the life from her. "But you figured I'd be home soon?" Her mouth curved downwards. The skin of her face darkened as if something were seeping up, staining it from beneath.

"That's not exactly it," Timmy said. He knew what he meant, but it wasn't something he could talk about.

"Well then?"

Ellen pulled on Pat's hand. "Mumma, guess what?"

"She's a girl," Timmy said.

"She's your daughter," Pat said, pulling her hand away from Ellen.

"I know that. That's the point." He felt frustration bristle up his back like a ridge of hair rising.

"Mumma," Ellen said. Pat made a shushing motion with her hand, her eyes riveted on Timmy. "No, the point is you made her sit in shit because you didn't want to get your hands dirty." She unshouldered her blue cloth bag and tossed it on the couch. A stack of 'Katie's Gonna Win' flyers slid out to spread across the rug.

Ellen slumped to the floor. "All you do is yell at each other and you never ever ever listen to me." She started to cry, her sobs half-swallowed.

Timmy watched as Pat bent down, put her hand to Ellen's back. "It's just a little argument. Everyone fights; it don't mean nothing," Pat said.

"But I don't want you to fight anymore." She wailed, lifting a face wet with tears. Her small mouth was loose and trembling so hard Timmy wanted to run from the room.

"I can change Katie, only don't fight," Ellen said, and she made to rise.

Timmy stood without being able to look either of them in the eyes. "No, I'll do it," he said. He gripped Katie's wheelchair, his palms sweaty on the plastic handles. Two minutes ago everyone was smiling. Now look at my home, what I've done, he thought. What good am I doing here? They'd be happier without me. He wheeled Katie towards the stairs.

Upstairs, he stretched her on her bed, having placed newspapers beneath her first, to catch anything that might spill. The smell told him it was diarrhea.

Timmy pulled her slacks off, untaped her diapers, and kept his face steady, fighting the urge to pull back. He held his breath and cleaned her legs, her bum, with wipies, then started on the front, rubbing and pulling at the mess caught in the small vee of her pubic hair. This is what he'd tried to explain to Pat, he thought, as he spread Katie's legs apart so he could clean out her vagina. He hated that, had always felt sick about it, even when she was a baby. He understood the need to clean her out, that you couldn't leave shit in there, but no matter how delicately he touched her, he always felt like a child molester.

Now that she was older, and her opening larger, he sometimes had to poke more of his finger in, to get her clean.

She's almost a teenager, for God's sake, he thought. No father should be putting his finger inside his teenager's vagina. No father should even know what his teenage daughter's vagina looked like.

It didn't help that Timmy understood he had no sexual feelings towards Katie, knew that this was as necessary for Katie's health as cleaning a wound. He still felt he was being forced to do something he had never wanted to do, never in a million years considered he would ever, ever have to do.

But that was pretty much the case with everything these days, he thought. His life was full of requirements no man could ever have anticipated. He listened to Pat's footsteps on the stairs. She was limping more these days, and he was worried about that, too? What if she broke down? Where would the money come from?

Pat entered the room with a tentativeness he knew was a gesture of truce. "You sure you don't want to come to the volunteers' luncheon even for a minute?" she asked from the doorway.

"The volunteer luncheon is today?" he asked.

"Timmy?" she said. "We talked about it this morning."

"I'm sorry. I forgot." The volunteer luncheon was a yearly event, a small way to say thank you to those who helped them with Katie. From the first, they'd both agreed they would always find a way to afford it. "Even if we have to steal or rob," Pat had said that first year Katie was home. This year, they'd told the owner of the restaurant that Timmy's parents would be sending a check directly to the restaurant. The owner, a small, roundish Italian with winglike clumps of hair frizzing out above his ears, said nothing when they told him. It was obvious he didn't believe a check would arrive in the mail any more than they believed it.

Timmy shook his head to Pat. "It's unemployment day,

and I want to go downtown to see if any of the stores are hiring for Christmas." Really, he didn't want to face the volunteers. They were too nice, willing and eager to work with Katie without the grudgingness, the desperate hope, Timmy brought to the task. And they didn't mind being seen with Katie in public. They felt no shame at the way people stared. All his life, Timmy had been the guy who faded into the background. He was comfortable there. Everyone left him alone, expected nothing. But now, out in public with Katie, he felt the stares and avoided gazes as if they were expectations. He didn't know what he was being called on to say or do. And when Pat acted like Katie could understand, talking to her like she was normal, Timmy had trouble hiding his discomfort and embarrassment. It didn't help that Pat gave him looks for not speaking to Katie himself. But how could he? Katie might as well be on the moon. And if he didn't talk to her, what would all the other people think? That he was a horrible father because he couldn't smile and coo at her like the volunteers would? How could he possibly explain to Pat that he couldn't go and still retain what little self-respect he had left?

Timmy turned to Pat now, hoping she'd take the wipie from his hand and finish the job. She turned away, descended the stairs. He pulled another wipie from its plastic can, then pushed Katie's legs apart so he could get in there. He was repulsed and humiliated by all the necessary moments of his life.

The long, fluorescent tubes overhead hummed like a gathering swarm of hornets. A typewriter clacked distantly from the rear of the office. No one in line spoke. Timmy could sense their stares, hear an occasional whisper—not a conversation, just a stab of words, a short, dry thrust of sound like a knife in sand. It was about him, he thought. They were all waiting to see what would happen when it was his turn.

This time the girl hesitated. The slight smirk she wore as she lifted her gaze from his card to Timmy, disappeared when she saw his expression. He could hear a slight waver in her voice as she said, "It's still missing, misplaced." His vision narrowed to focus on her lips, covered with a thick, orange lipstick. The lipstick was smeared slightly on the right side of her mouth. A fleck of it dotted the tip of her tongue, so that he watched an orange spot flicker at him as she spoke.

"Where's the boss?" Timmy asked.

She turned and he shifted to look at the empty desk with her. She waited for several seconds, as if hoping he might appear, before telling Timmy, "He's on vacation."

"Vacation?" he nearly shouted. A low moan of outrage rose from the people behind him in line.

"I'm sure, when he gets back..."

"No," Timmy said. "No." He squeezed the counter with his hands. His arms and legs shook. It felt like the muscles in his neck might burst. His face heated and he tried not to think of the sweat sheeting from his skin. "Look," he said, his voice harsh, breathy, but strangely quiet. "All I want is the money that I worked for. I am sorry if I said something to piss you people off. But that's my money and it's right there." When he pointed his finger at the supervisor's desk, his gaze landed on a manilla file set in a vertical holder in the same place his file had been placed that first week. Before he knew it was happening, he was pushing through the gate, past the astonished faces of the people at the other desks, beyond the tentative commands that he stop. He felt a hand grip his forearm, glanced down to notice white skin, nails painted orange, and he continued moving forward, pulling her with him, until he was at the desk and his hands were on the file. His name, printed on a white gummed label, looked up at him from the top of the folder. "That's me," he said. "This is me." He opened the folder to the woman, feeling his stomach turn at the few slight pages contained within.

"I can't help you, there are certain procedures," she went on to explain. Her voice was a soft drone, pleading for understanding, and he missed most of what she said as he stared at the meager facts of his life.

Timmy closed the folder, poked his finger on the name

tag, tapped it. "That's me." He motioned tentatively at the desk. "I've been here the whole time."

"Mr. Kingchester will be back from vacation next week," she said.

Timmy became enraged at the sound of the man's name. "I've got a family. I've got a wife, I've got two daughters, one of them is brain damaged..." His voice caught and he had to swallow, force himself to go on. "We are so goddamn broke...I'm going to food pantries...I've picked up bottles on the street...I can't get out of goddamned bed. I want...I just want..." He thrust his hands up towards the ceiling and turned towards the others in line. It was like he could see all their eyes looking at him with sympathy and understanding. "Do I have to have a gun to get what's mine?" Timmy said in a voice ragged with grief. The people in line nodded, muttered assents as if saying Amens.

The woman looked at him, her mouth somehow softer, her cheeks sucked in. She opened his file as if looking through it. Timmy could tell she was just pretending. She didn't want to look at his face. "You got kids," he said. "Don't you?"

She nodded. He watched her swallow. Her tongue came out to wet her lips and her forehead wrinkled with the concentration of thought.

"I did my job," Timmy said. "It ain't my fault the plant closed. You think I like to be here?"

The woman shut her eyes. "This job sucks." She opened her eyes and tipped her face up, as if wanting Timmy to examine it. "I'm not like this outside of here, believe me." She looked back at the folder, closed it. "I don't know what the hell I can do. But I'll do something."

"What?" Timmy asked, but she looked away.

Her short hair swung in a curve around one ear, then the other, as she shook her head. "I'm sorry. I really am sorry. But...I can't give you a check without my boss' approval. When he gets back, I'll talk to him. He's got to listen..."

For some reasons Timmy thought of the 1979 Pittsburgh

Pirates, World Champions, with their theme song, "We Are Family." That was only ten years ago, but Timmy couldn't for his life picture that happening here now, today. "This whole damn city is sorry," he said. He left with his head down, not looking at anyone.

Chapter 14

WE HELD the annual volunteer's luncheon at the usual place, Dominic's. It's only a few blocks from the house, so I was able to wheel Katie there without much trouble. Only fourteen people had signed up to go. When I first complained to Timmy about it, he told me, "People got their own families, too." Of course, he didn't make it either. I understood. But I'd be lying if I didn't say I was disappointed. I mean, these people, they were our family, because we laughed together, we cried together, and we helped each other out in times we were sick.

I'd reserved the downstairs function room, and I watched nervously as two dishwashers carried Katie down the winding steps, handling her as if she were a sack of flour. They settled her into the wheelchair at the end of the long table. Actually, sort of dumped her in it. "Be careful, she's a little girl," I said.

One guy, a thin, cross-eyed man with a narrow chin and skin the color of weak tea, put his hands up as if I were holding a gun to him. "Hey, we didn't touch her."

I sat in the chair without looking at him, I was so embarrassed. I don't know if I was embarrassed because he'd misunderstood me, or because Katie was getting to the age where people would even be thinking about touching her in that way.

Anyways, I almost felt like a Mafia boss, sitting there. The way people came by to pay their respect. One by one the volunteers stopped down to touch Katie's hair, say a few cheerful words to her, or to tell me she was doing better. Mary Catherine pinned a small snowman onto Katie's purple sweater and said, "She's happy today." As if that were enough. That disconcerted me, although I tried to keep smiling. Mary Catherine might be right. I didn't know if I was ready for that.

I watched Katie smile and stare at the tray of her chair. Her head was cocked and her eyes distant, like she was listening to someone whisper in her ear.

"She's happy because she doesn't have to do the program," I said. "She's just a big, lazy bunny." I smiled at Katie, as if sharing a joke with her. She swayed her head from side to side and lifted her fingers to her mouth to suck on them.

"Quit it. You're a big girl," I told her, moving her hand away. She made grasping motions with her lips.

I opened the glossy menu and held it before her face. "What do you want?" I asked. As if repeating her answer, I said, "A hamburger? Good. What do you want on that? Lettuce and tomato? Good."

From the other end of the table came a laugh as small and bright as two marbles clacking together. Ellen was sitting beside Mary Catherine, who'd made a puppet out of her napkin and was tweaking Ellen's nose with it. I looked at the empty chair to my right and felt abandoned.

"Ellen, come sit by me," I said.

She pouted and slumped deep in her chair. "Do I have to?"

I tried to laugh, to pretend it was no big deal, but I could feel my face redden. Someone to my left said, "Kids."

Mary Catherine folded the napkin and set it in her lap. She told Ellen, "Go on honey. Sit beside your mother."

Ellen sullenly scuffed her way over and slouched heavily against the curved back of the chair.

I felt as awkward as I had back in the fifth grade, the time my family moved, on that first day in a new school, having to talk to kids I'd never known in my life. But this was my daughter.

What was wrong with me? I felt like one of those women you read about who lock their kids in the closet because they're too busy to take care of them. Jesus Pat, I thought. I wondered how those women libbers did it, working full time and everything. I was home all day and I still couldn't take care of my whole family.

"So," I said. "You get a day off school today, huh?" I smiled. Ellen shrugged.

I checked Katie. Her hand was in her mouth. I took it out and slid it beneath the tray of her chair, knowing she'd have a difficult time moving it out from there. Behind my water glass, there was a cut-glass vase full of breadsticks. I took one, broke off a piece, and placed it on Katie's tongue. She mashed it against the roof of her mouth.

All around the table, the bright, animated voices of the volunteers seemed a kind of mocking. For a second, I hated them. I wanted to yell, "Shut up. You have no right to be happy until Katie gets better." I was ashamed at myself for feeling that way. They had every right. They were people, too. I heard Ellen squirm in her chair and turned to her. She looked so bored and unhappy. It struck me then—I was the one doing that to her. I remembered some of the things I'd talked about with Shirley.

I broke another chunk from the breadstick. "Here it comes," I said, zooming it like an airplane at her mouth.She looked at me, shocked. "Mumma?" she said.

"Get ready," I told her. "Yeeeooooww, it's delicious." I flew it past her lips. She unfolded her arms and pushed herself straighter in the seat. Her lips parted in anticipation.

"You got to catch it now," I told her. I made a figure eight in the air, then dove down towards her mouth. Ellen snapped at the breadstick and bit my fingers.

"Oww," I said. "Jeez! What are you, a cannibal?"

She laughed and took my hand and pretended to chomp on it. I felt an inner lightening, a freshness, like I'd just opened a window in a stale room to let in some air.

Then I felt the nagging pull of guilt and I turned to Katie. She was slumped forward, her mouth open, trying to taste her vanished hand. I leaned over to do something. But, you know, she looked totally content. I looked back at my other daughter.

"Do that again, Mumma," Ellen said. She squeezed my hand. I had to fight the impulse to draw it back.

I broke off another piece of breadstick, performed dips and loops with it, teased it away from Ellen several times before I let her nibble it gently into her mouth. She gave my fingertips a big stage kiss and I felt like crying.

"Now let me do it to you," she said. I felt awkward, foolish, like a big baby. But when Ellen started to break off bits and feed me, I felt like I could sit there all day, taking this bread from her small, sweet-smelling hands. I couldn't remember the last time something this nice had happened to me—the last time I had let something happen.

It was the best luncheon. People were talking and laughing. Near the end, we sang a couple old Beatle songs. Ellen stood up and did some kind of rap dance and everyone laughed. Even the food. To tell you the truth, I always thought the food there was about the level of Chef Boyardee. But some people ordered seconds.

I thought, this is it, things are turning, your life is going to get better Pat. You just have to learn to relax a bit. I made this little pact with God; as long as I was a good girl, and stopped yelling at people and tried to be nicer, Katie would get well. That's what the problem was, I wasn't being nice enough to everyone else. I thought of Timmy, and got this sort of twinge in my heart. Shirley had hit the nail on the head. I'd been expecting too much from him. He wasn't the tough guy everyone thinks when they see someone in a blue workshirt. He could break in a second, just like anyone. I should've known that. I should've been paying closer attention to what he was going through, too.

All right, I told myself. I would change. Be more patient and understanding. Forgiving. He didn't ask for the plant to close. He didn't want everyone to tell him he wasn't good enough, or smart enough, or wasn't whatever, just wasn't enough, every time he went for a job. He didn't ask them to screw up his unemployment checks. He didn't need more grief at home.

Thinking about all this in that room, with the volunteers, my happy family, around me, it felt like I was being cleansed or something. Like all this bad stuff was being washed away. With that, I felt a new hope in my heart. This would be the start of it. Not the start of a new life, so much, as a return to our old one. That's what I'd needed all along—to straighten myself out. Thank you God, I prayed in my head, thank You for straightening my ass out. I looked over at Katie. Breadstick crumbs stuck to her bottom lip, speckled her chin. I was certain that it was only a matter of time before she'd be normal again. She'd turn her face to me, smile, say "Mumma," and get up and walk. I took her home that afternoon and I was happier, more confident she'd get better, than at any time I could remember. Then, that night, I saw the blood.

Chapter 15

ACCORDING TO A PLAQUE on the pillar at the downtown end, the Sixth Street Bridge had won an award in 1928 for its beauty. It was a solid-looking bridge, with bands of steel looping up and down from its two towers as if the bands were suspension cables. The bridge was painted a dull yellow which looked sickly against the cloud-packed Pittsburgh sky. As Timmy walked across it, moving aimlessly, a gust of wind shook him so that he grabbed the cold railing for support. Below him, the water of the Allegheny River was a choppy gray-green. There were no boats out today, but one man was fishing. He stood in the parking lot which flanked the river like an asphalt cuff along the downtown side. His hands were sunk into the pockets of his dungaree jacket, the pole trapped between his right elbow and his ribs. When he saw Timmy looking, the man shrugged, as if to acknowledge his craziness, or desperation. Timmy turned away.

He looked upriver at the criss-crossed lines of the other bridges. Then he shifted his attention to the city center, a mixture of new and old structures. The old buildings had round smokestacks and blackened walls. Their rough, worked-in look seemed to define the Pittsburgh that Timmy had grown up in. But the new buildings, with their reflective windows and pointed roofs —one was topped by a jutting lance—their clean blue or salmon colored bricks, gleaming like marble under the dark sky...They didn't seem real. They looked like toys. As he gazed at them, seeing the city reflected in slight distortions on their clean surfaces, Timmy was struck by how many thousands of windows there were down here. If he had all day he couldn't count them all. At least one person worked behind each window, he thought. One minimum. Who were they? What the hell did they do? Why couldn't he find a window to fit behind?

He headed across the river again, towards the North Side. North Shore the politicians wanted to call it now. What did they think, that by giving it a yuppie name they could make the regular people, the poor people, the working people, who lived there disappear?

The bridge emptied at a small park. There was a statue there of two working men. Surveyors, he guessed, looking back at the bridge. The man to Timmy's left carried an unfurled tube of plans in his right hand. His left foot rested on a tool box. In the spread fingers of his raised left hand, someone had stuck a cigarette butt. A tight, foamy ball of spittle clung to the chin of that statue's face.

The other statue held a tripod in its right hand. Its left hand was bent at the wrist and set on his hip, making a triangle from his body into which someone had tucked a red and white popcorn box.

In the past, something like this would've outraged Timmy. Today he thought, that about sums it up; the new Pittsburgh. The new thanks-for-your-help-fuck-you Pittsburgh. It made him sick.

Timmy followed a small spit of grass which ran along the river towards Three Rivers Stadium. He believed this was called Roberto Clemente Park, named after the Pirates' great right fielder, who had died in a plane crash while bringing food to earthquake victims in Nicaragua. It wasn't much of a memorial. But then again, Clemente wasn't white. Timmy couldn't recall a single statue in the city honoring a person who wasn't white. A phrase ran through his head—*howsoever you treat the least of these*. Then, what goes around comes around. He couldn't quite explain it, but he had the feeling that he, and others like him, had been somehow manipulated, made partners in their own deceit.

At the Stadium, he crossed the parking lot where he'd often tailgated at Steelers' games; grilling burgers, quaffing beers with thousands of others, sometimes getting there four or five hours before kick-off, everyone partying, screaming, whooping, the noise growing so loud you couldn't hold a conversation—not that anyone wanted to. But today the lot was empty, except for the wind which hummed as it whipped across the asphalt. Timmy shoved his hands in the pockets of his denim jacket and hunched lower as he headed for the bridge which would bring him back across the river to Point State Park, the triangular grassy field where, in the summer, his father used to bring Timmy to play by the fountain when the weather was muggy. Then, when Timmy became a father, he brought his kids.

He remembered the first time he'd brought Katie, she'd laughed so hard as she raced around the fountain's concrete base, she actually threw up. But she kept on running, circling, coming back to Timmy only when the mist from the thirty foot spray of water caught her face and she needed her eyes wiped. She must've been three at the time, because he could picture her moving in that loose, limb-flung way, as if her arms and legs were all double-jointed. God, he'd give anything to see her do that now. He still couldn't believe what had happened to her. Sometimes, looking at her, he was reminded of a story Pat's father used to tell, about leprechauns stealing into a house, removing the baby from the crib, and leaving another creature, a changeling, in the baby's place. If you were a Christian, Pat's Dad would say, you would know that creature was from the other world, and you would take that changeling out into the woods, leave it there, and pray to God that the leprechauns would bring it back to the world where it belonged.

He cut through the park, hurrying now, as if there were something chasing him. Entering the busy city streets, he felt assaulted by noise. The sounds of trucks and buses set up a constant dull roar. He decided to turn right, head for the Boulevard of the Allies, maybe take a look at the Monongahela

River. He approached a church, St. Mary's, and hesitated. He considered entering. He hadn't been to church since Katie first took sick.

Timmy looked now at the welcoming arms of the cement statue of the Virgin set above the door of St. Mary's. Maybe, he thought, there was still some hope, something he could believe in, if he gave it one more try. But as he looked at the Virgin's welcoming gesture, he remembered the woman at the massage parlor, opening her arms to encourage Timmy inside. She'd guided him into a small cubicle dominated by a vinyl-topped table, stripped him, then herself, and all the time she was working on him they talked about kids, his, then hers. "I don't tell them what I do," she said, and he let her still do it, trying to convince himself that her quick stroking was an act of intimacy, bringing them closer, a kind of grace.

It wasn't until she handed him a face cloth to clean himself off that he'd been overpowered by the degradation of it all, recognized just what kind of man he was, and had slumped to the floor, sobbing so hard, she was the one who had somehow gotten him dressed, pushed him out the door, and even guided him to an Eat'n Park restaurant where he spent the night drinking coffee and weeping until he'd scared everyone else out and so had the place to himself.

Certainly, he wasn't worthy to go into any church.

He hurried to the corner, took a left up the Boulevard of the Allies. A long line of men momentarily halted his progress. There were old men, their faces grizzled and doughy, with noses like doorknobs; young black men wearing vinyl jackets over sweatshirts whose hoods were pulled up. A woman in a bright red kerchief and damp-looking corduroy coat said to Timmy, "I think we got something hot today. Someone said soup." Her lips were lost in her sunken mouth, and as she set the two cardboard-handled shopping bags she carried to the sidewalk, the bags frayed and stuffed full of clothing, cans, and what looked to be an old, gray furry seal, she rubbed her arms and asked, "What shelter you at?"

Timmy, gripped with horror, ran past the line, past the red door where the food was being dispensed, into the street—horns blaring at him—and kept running until he reached Smithfield Street, and started across that bridge.

The Smithfield Street bridge is a low structure, close to the water. The walkway is made of steel grating, and it shook beneath Timmy as the traffic passed. On the roadbed, the tar was worn down in large patches to its steel weave. The bridge itself was a faded silver, full of fist-sized rivets, and featuring long, looping bands which roller-coastered upwards and downwards in crossing lines which assumed the illusion of cables.

The water here, in the Monongaheala River, was calmer, more a muddy green, pale and whitened and full of blackened tree limbs and debris. In the wharf parking lot close to the city, cars crowded the bank like lemmings too apathetic to throw themselves in, only waiting for the water to rise and sweep them away.

Across the way stood Station Square, a development of expensive shops and restaurants Timmy could never afford to eat in. It was an old railroad station that had been redone. The main building was a seven-story brick structure, longer than it was tall, fronted by disused trolley cars and the still functioning railroad tracks. To Timmy, it looked like some gigantic lozenge aerated by burnished windows so large the interior, he guessed, would be full of light. To the left, the old P & LERR building rose its shabby, yellow bricks, an **OFFICES AVAILABLE** banner strung just beneath its flat roof. Anchoring the far end of the development was the Sheraton, with its encircled red *S* like a badge on its side. On the banks before the hotel, a small flotilla of white river boats, strung, even in daytime, with popcorn lines of yellow lights, waited to take people drinking, dancing, or sight-seeing, to view the decayed hulks of mills and warehouses which had made this city distinct; had made it Pittsburgh, and not someplace else.

All of this, Timmy thought, looking from Station Square back to the buildings of downtown...all of this had been built by people like him. They had used his kind to put up these places to hire people who were nothing like him. The city had used them, he thought. Used them to build a new city, a city with walls, ramparts, and fortresses which they, the people who'd built them, would never be allowed to broach. They used us, Timmy thought, to build a city where working people would be obsolete.

As far up and down river as he could see, bridges spanned the river, connecting the neighborhoods where people lived with the city center where business occured. Once, those bridges had seemed solid to Timmy. Now they were like loose stitches holding together downtown and the South Side slopes, with its apartment buildings cramped shoulder to shoulder in a staggering mob that clung to the hills, and its streets full of unemployed men and cheap barrooms. For what reason were these bridges still up? He watched the traffic crossing, cars, buses, and trolleys, the people coming from furthur away, going home to more distant suburbs, while the people close by were left to rot. These bridges once stiched together Pittsburgh's past and future, but now, he thought, there was no way to bring those two sides together. And so his present had become a nightmare. His only hope of escape lie in pulling something as rash and irrational as Gerry had proposed. And the risk? He thought about all that had happened to him these past few years, what he'd become. Maybe there was no risk. Maybe Pat, Katie, and Ellen would be better off without him anyways.

Chapter 16

AFTER LUNCH, Katie was in a strange mood—sort of confused, grouchy, and scared. It must be the food, I thought at first. But it kept on, all through the afternoon and into supper. Timmy never came home after Unemployment. It was his turn to cook, too, and it was weird, him not showing up, not calling. When Ellen asked me, though, "Where's Daddy?" I tried to pretend it was no big deal that he was missing.

"Oh, he's probably at a friend's," I told her.

"But he always comes home for supper."

"Not always," I said.

Ellen was standing behind me while I washed the chicken legs off in the sink. I'd waited as long as I could and now everyone was so starving I figured I'd have to boil it. "Name me one time," she said.

I turned, suddenly angry, but she was smiling, so I put a good face on and shook a piece of chicken at her. "You want this in your puss?"

"Ooo yuck, Mumma!" she said. "You got chicken juice on me." She wiped at her eyes with the heels of her hands.

"How's about I get some in your hair?" I raised the pale yellow leg as if it were one of those shaking instruments Indians on TV use for their rain dances. "Give you a nice chicken juice rinse."

"Yikes," she screamed, laughing as she ran into the living room and dove onto the couch. I heard her asking Katie, "Do you want to watch Duck Tales, too?" Katie moaned, a low creak seeming to come from her belly. "Mumma, I think something's wrong with Katie," Ellen said.

I looked at her from the doorway. She was hunched over more than usual. "She's just tired," I said without conviction. I returned to the kitchen and dropped the chicken, a few potatoes and a couple pieces of cut up carrots into a pot, then ran water from the faucet to cover it.

It wasn't like Timmy to do this. I began to wonder if maybe he'd gotten his check and gone down to Harry's to celebrate. I'll kill him, I told myself, if he's drinking it all up.

But it wasn't like Timmy to do something like that, either. So I began to think maybe he didn't get his check and was too depressed to face us. But neither was that like Timmy. I started thinking about how he'd been that morning, before we'd left for Dominic's. He'd played Candyland three times with Ellen. He'd actually taken Katie out of her chair and rocked her in his lap. And when he went to leave, he looked at me and his eyes all teared up. I couldn't handle it, so I turned away before he tried to hold me.

None of that was like Timmy, the Timmy I knew. Or was it? I mean, if he was doing it, it was like him. Wasn't it? Maybe he was changing and I just hadn't noticed. Maybe I was making him into something in my mind that he wasn't really like. Maybe I wasn't seeing clearly. I thought hard about his actions again. It was like shades were pulled back from behind my eyes and this light streamed in. He'd acted, that morning, like somebody saying Good-bye. Was he leaving me? Had he, my God, had it?

Oh shit, I thought. That was the last thing I needed at this moment in my life.

When the volunteers started arriving for that night's program, it was like they all knew. Every single one asked me the same thing, "Where's Timmy?"

"I don't know," I said. "I don't know. Let's just get this

program on the road."

Alex helped me bring Katie down to the cellar and put her on the table. Before we even started, she gave out this long, low cry like I never heard from her; sort of like the sound you might hear from a Siamese cat in pain. I told the volunteers that maybe it was just her diaper was wet or something, giving her a rash. My stomach was twisting itself around. I didn't believe it, but I decided to change her before we began, see if that helped. I pulled the tape loose, folded the Huggie down flat to the table, and saw it; mixed with the greenish spread of her urine was the unmistakeable stain of Katie's first period.

"Get out, go home, just get out of here," I told the volunteers. A few of them paused, questions on their lips, and I said, "Don't even ask." Mary Catherine touched my shoulder on the way out. "You have my number," she said. "If you need to talk, don't be afraid, even if it's three in the morning." I almost hugged her right then, and I think she knew it. She leaned over and gave me a kiss on the cheek and turned away so I wouldn't have to worry about her seeing me cry.

I cleaned Katie up and fixed her with a pad from the box I kept hidden in the closet down here so Ellen wouldn't find them and ask me what they were before I was ready to tell her. Ellen, I thought, oh God, she's up there all by herself. I felt the urge to hold her, as if she needed protection from something. But what could I do? I couldn't leave Katie. In that second, I felt a furious rush of hatred for Timmy, for not being there. Only I couldn't hold onto it. I started muttering, crying to myself, "This isn't how it's supposed to be." I moved Katie to the rug, almost dropping her when my knee gave out, and sat, cradling her head in my lap, rocking and crying for God knows how long. I felt like I'd reached a limit of some sort. Like someone had been putting me through these tests and I'd finally failed. Like I'd been fooling myself, thinking I was in control.

When I was able to calm down a bit, clean my face off with my hand, I called up to Ellen, "Come down here for a second, will you?"

She lingered at the doorway, her attention still on the TV. I said nothing. I knew she'd turn towards me when a commercial came on. I heard a louder flare of sound, and Ellen turned, bounced halfway down the stairs. She smiled at me and asked, "Do you know what Johnny Nelson said to me the other day?" She looked closely at me and Katie and said, "What are you doing?"

"I'm playing with your sister," I said.

She cocked her head, skeptical.

"Did you finish your homework?" I asked, knowing that would stop her from looking at me.

She lifted her arms above her head, rose up on her toes, and turned in a circle.

"Stop that," I told her. "How many times I have to tell you not to play on the stairs? I can't take care of two of you."

"Oh Mumma," she said, lowering her feet flat. she shook her head, opened her eyes wide, and, waving her arms, pretended she was falling.

"That's not funny," I said. She smacked her lips and stood, waiting. The air around me seemed full of dust and silence. "What did Johnny Nelson say?"

"He said," she leaned forward, gripped the railing, and shook her bum. "He said that he used to have a sister but she got retarded and now she lives in a hospital and his father says she's not his sister anymore."

"His father's an asshole."

Ellen stepped back to lean against the wall. She placed her hand over her mouth. "You said a bad word."

"You want to hear another?" I said. She smiled, happy to have a secret to connect us.

"Katie's always going to be your sister," I said.

"I know that," Ellen told me impatiently.

"Even if she never gets better..." My voice caught. I looked away and waved my hand to Ellen, for her to leave.

"I'm glad," she said quietly, but with conviction. Then she giggled. "He also said I'm cute," she added, swirling her skirt. She turned and started to scamper up the stairs.

"Wait," I called. I couldn't see her, but I heard her stop moving. She must've been about ready to shut the door. "Ring up Shirley and ask her to come over."

"Shirley?"

"Tell her it's important. I need her to help me carry Katie up the stairs. The number's on the sheet by the phone."

"Mumma, I'm not a baby, I know that," she told me. "I'm a big girl now."

I looked at Katie; "Yes you are honey. Yes you are."

I stroked Katie's hair, brushed it back off her furrowed forehead. Six-years-old, and Ellen's already thinking of boys, I thought. "God help us," I said, smiling at Katie. I started to explain to her about periods, and pregnancy, and being a woman. "Someday, you're going to have a boyfriend..." A sob caught in my throat. "Someday you'll sit down with your own daughter and talk to her just like I'm talking to you..." I was crying so hard it felt like my body was emptying out, like I wouldn't be finished until there was nothing more inside. And I was scared, because, what would happen then? What if, when I was done, I really was empty, I had nothing more to give her?

For some reason, I started thinking about church, some of the stories the priest read to us from the Bible. There were stories about Jesus healing these cripples, and guys with leprosy, and sluts. I couldn't help thinking how unfair that was. What's wrong with my Katie? She's just a little girl, for crying out loud. Why does she have to suffer like this? "What do you want from her?" I said softly, then I was yelling, "What do you want from me? Who the hell are You?" In the musty closeness of the cellar, the words came back to me, a slight echo.

"Just a local bag lady," Shirley said, clumping heavily down the stairs. She had a cigarette in her mouth, but it had been stubbed out. When she saw my face, she took the cigarette out, dropped it in the pocket of her blue workshirt, and said, "What is it?"

"Just help me carry Katie up, please."

149

Shirley bent, touched Katie's forehead. "She's sweaty." She positioned herself to take Katie beneath the arms. "Where are your volunteers?"

"I sent them home." I couldn't look at her eyes just yet. It felt like I was trying to build up the breath in my lungs to tell her.

"Where's Timmy?"

"I don't know. I don't know anymore. I don't know where I am anymore."

"Hey meatball," she said.

"Shirley." I looked right at her then. "Katie's a woman now," I said. Shirley's eyes seemed to sharpen slowly as it became clear to her. "She got the curse."

"I'll take Ellen across to play with Jimmy Junior—Jim's home—and then I'll come back and we'll talk."

"Thanks," I said.

"Thanks nothing," she said, jerking her head back to let me know she was ready to start up the stairs. "Wait'll you see my bill."

It was enough to get me to smile.

Chapter 17

"YOU KNOW WHAT'S FUNNY about being out of work?" Gerry said. He drove west down Walnut Street, through the Shadyside section of Pittsburgh, an upscale neighborhood of clothing boutiques, jewelry stores, and restaurants. On the sidewalk to his left, a young, dark-haired woman in a mini-skirt and leather jacket was looking at a Vietnamese pig in the window of a pet store. Gerry shook his head. "This place used to be all hippies. Then the government money came in—supposedly so people could rehab these dumps and have affordable places to live. Now look at it." He snorted. "Can't buy an *apartment* for under two grand."

Timmy shifted his feet around the duffel bag on the floor. The scent of the flowers in the back seat made his stomach queasy, but the flowers were their ticket in. As Gerry said, "Who's not going to open their door for a flower delivery?" They were headed for a condo owned by Jake Brewer, a hot-shot local businessman who owned a string of pizzerias. From what Timmy recalled of Brewer, seeing him in the paper or on TV, he was a short, fat energetic man, with a bald head and a face shaped like the rump of a small, hairless burrowing animal. According to Gerry, he and the mayor were lovers. "She's seventy years old," Timmy had protested, "she can't have a lover."

Gerry had smiled then. In his reflective sunglasses, Timmy saw two distorted images of his own pained face. "Can and does," Gerry said. "And she's waiting there tonight for him to come back to Pittsburgh on a red-eye flight."

"How do you know all this?"

"Money talks," Gerry said. "Well, liquor does." Timmy gave him a puzzled look. Gerry nodded his beard upwards. "I know this kid, Mike Vargo, plays in a rock band with Brewer's son. Get Vargo loaded and he'll blab about anything. Hell, if I had some pot, he probably could've got me photos of Jake and the mayor in a hot tub."

Timmy squinted out the window now as they halted at a stop light. Across the street, a man wearing wool slacks and a gray and green sweater knitted in angular, geometric designs, pulled money from an automatic teller machine. Timmy and Pat had closed their bank account months ago to save the $5 monthly fee.

Gerry took a right onto Aiken Avenue, into a line of traffic. His headlights illuminated the bumper stickers on the car in front of them. Justice for El Salvador. Save the Whales. The Thomas Merton Center. Justice for Pittsburgh, he thought. Save me. Who the hell is Thomas Merton?

Remembering the start of this conversation, he looked over at Gerry. "Weren't you just talking about what's funny about being out of work?"

Gerry tipped his head back. He tried to laugh in a hearty, fearless manner, as if they were two guys going out for a beer. But his voice was strained.

Gerry took a left onto Centre Avenue and parked the car at the fifth meter on the right. They were beside a brown brick highrise. Across the street, three double streetlights cast an orange haze through the Food Gallery parking lot. Pools of light spilled onto the rows of cars in front of the store. Timmy watched people rushing out of the store with carts and armloads full of groceries. You could bet they weren't buying generic crap; day-old bread; no-name spaghetti; canned pork that tasted like metal.

"When I was working," Gerry said, pulling the key from the ignition, "I knew the Steelers' schedule cold. I knew when draft day was, and when the spring drills began. I knew the

Pirates' homestands a month ahead, and I even knew when the Penguins played on TV. I knew when the newspapers were going to run columns, previews, and wrap-ups. I followed the sports reports on TV, and listened to the radio talk shows. It was like, these teams...I kept track of my life by them."

Rain started to fall intermittently, a few drops streaking the windshield in a dotted line, then there was a quick burst, the drops making a loud, metallic pattering on the roof. Then it stopped.

Gerry was ticking things off on his fingers. "Steelers, Pirates, Post-Gazette, Pittsburgh Press, KDKA, WTAE, my job, and Harry's. That was me. I knew where I was, and when it was, and what was going on. Do you see what I'm saying?"

Timmy pulled his chin into his chest. He looked at their meter, which showed a yellow half circle that said EXPIRED. He wondered if they needed to put money in it. The craziness of worrying about that caused him to laugh out loud.

"Yeah, so I wasn't saving the world. It was a life." Gerry opened his hands, palms up, on the steering wheel. Timmy was surprised to see how small his fingers were. "I felt a part of things. Now, if the Steelers win—so what? If I don't read the paper one day—what of it? I feel like I don't live in this city, like I ain't connected with other people any more. Yeah, there's the guys at Harry's, but it's not the same as arguing at work about Smizak's column one day, and then what Steigerwald said on TV the next day, then betting in the pool on Friday, and getting all excited with waiting on Saturday, and knowing on Sunday that all the buddies you'd be seeing on Monday were doing the same thing as you and you'd have something to talk about, something you sort of did together." He reached down past Timmy's leg for the duffel bag and set it in his lap with a sigh. "Back in high school, we used to think, man wouldn't it be great to find a doctor who could write a note, get you on disability, so you wouldn't have to work, your time would be your own. But, I don't know about that. When you ain't working, what's a Monday? What's a weekend? What's important?"

Gerry tucked his beard into the collar of his black jacket and buttoned the top button. "I feel like I don't belong nowhere. Like this city is going on, living some kind of life without me. I don't have no part in it no more. I'm the fucking invisible man, you know? I ain't real."

Timmy watched as another burst of rain swept down, blurring the windshield so that the lights of the cars driving towards them became long, wavery smears of yellow. "You know what we are?" he said to Gerry. "We're nothing. We're nobody. We're little people, you know? The kind nobody ever thinks about because, really, what have we got to say to anyone? Who gives a shit about us? We're not going to be heroes. We're going to be fucking bums."

He looked over for Gerry's response. Gerry sat still, not looking back at him, for close to a minute. Then he took a nylon mask from the bag, then a black luger. "I'm sick of your pussy-assed shit," he said, raising the barrel to Timmy's face. Timmy jumped in his seat. A sensation like small, clawed feet scrabbled up the inside of his chest. "You said no weapons," he whispered in a high, tight voice.

Gerry pulled the trigger. A squirt of water caught Timmy in the eye. He laughed. Timmy rubbed his face dry with his hand and called Gerry a jerk.

"That old bag won't know it ain't real," Gerry said. He nudged Timmy's shoulder. "C'mon. Loosen up." He ducked out of the car and opened the back door for the flowers. "Trust me, once we get inside, the rest is gravy."

Mayor Stephanie Mendelson sat on the rust-colored velour couch, her arms crossed defiantly. She wore a pair of white flannel pajamas decorated with tiny red roses, and furry red slippers. Her hair was suprisingly attractive, Timmy thought, thick and wavy, cut off her forehead and back behind her ears, its burnished orange color somehow making her small, pale-brown eyes appear more alert. She was a large woman, Gerry's size, and although the flesh on her cheeks sagged, the long, straight line of her jaw, her wide chin, gave her face a look of determination, so that when she stared at Timmy and said, "Why don't you deadbeats get out of town?" his first impulse was to leave.

Gerry waved the gun at her, then lowered it to his side. "Look, we'll carry you if we have to."

"You and whose Army?" she asked. She looked from Gerry to Timmy, who stood uncomfortably by the door, still holding the flowers. "It's six flights down. I weigh 182 pounds. And you won't fool Ron Crockett, the elevator operator, with that water pistol." She thrust her chin forward at Gerry.

Timmy and Gerry looked to see a slow stream of drops dripping from the gun barrel onto the gold carpeting.

"This city don't need deadbeats like you," she said.

Gerry fumed silently. Timmy felt called on to say something. "It ain't personal," he said. "I voted for you in the primaries."

Her mouth softened out of its puppetlike frown into a straight line. She turned to the coffee table on her left and lifted an Oreo cookie from a small pyramid of them arranged on a china plate. After carefully pulling the cookie apart, she proceeded to scrape the icing off with her bottom teeth.

Timmy told Gerry, "Let's forget this. I mean—look at her. She could be your Grandmom."

Gerry gave out a whine of complaint. "What's the matter with you?"

"You hush up," the mayor told him. "This is still a free city and he has a right to talk." She made a 'come here' motion with her hand to Timmy. He placed the flowers on the other end table, beside another small plate, this one stacked with a neat square made from bite-sized Clark bars, and went to stand before her. He felt like a little kid about to be scolded.

"What are you doing?" Gerry asked.

"She's an old lady." Timmy made a pleading gesture with his hands. "I'm just being polite."

The mayor smiled. "Hon? Who's going to care if you kidnap the mayor? I don't run things any more than the queen runs England. You get up this high in government and it's all realtors and businessmen pulling your strings."

"Hey? Cut the chit-chat. We got business here," Gerry said.

"I told you to hush," the mayor said. "Didn't your mother teach you any manners?" Gerry, who had moved close to Timmy, stepped back, uncertain what to do next.

The mayor told Timmy, "This is just a job."

"You can't be serious," Timmy said.

"This is ridiculous," Gerry threw his hands out. "Cut the crap, let's go. You, up. Off the couch."

Her mouth clenched tight. Only her lips moved as she said, "I bet you voted for Lucheesi in the primaries. That man is so deep in DeBartolini's pocket, he may as well be DeBartolini's underwear. You want this city run by someone from Ohio?"

"I didn't even vote," Gerry said.

"Then you have no right to complain," she told him.

"I'm not complaining. I'm kidnapping you." His voice was husky with frustration.

"I won't be kidnapped by someone who doesn't even vote."

Gerry take a step forward, and Timmy put his hand out for him to stop. "Look," Timmy told the mayor, "we're just gonna hold you, and ransom you back for two jobs."

She cocked her head, her look amused. Then she took another cookie, pulled it apart, and began scraping off the icing. Timmy noticed that the uneaten black cookie wafers were stacked like checkers on the lower tier of the coffee table.

"It's to highlight the plight of workers," Gerry said.

The mayor stopped scraping and slowly swallowed what was in her mouth. "Highlight? Plight? What are you running for City Council too? Are you Jimmy Ferlo? Is this a joke?"

"Get up now," Gerry said. "I mean it."

She turned to Timmy. "If you want to take a sandwich with you, there's some chipped ham in the fridge."

"I've had it," Gerry said. He thrust Timmy aside, grabbed

the mayor's arm, and yanked her to her feet. She bumped into him, knocking him back a foot. Her face turned blotchy, and her eyes showed fear now, and uncertainty, as if she really weren't sure what kind of danger she faced. Timmy knew that look. He'd seen it in Pat's eyes, in his own eyes in the mirror, whenever they talked about Katie. He felt suddenly beset by bone-deep weariness. "Let her go, Gerry," he said.

Gerry swung around to face him.

The mayor straightened her pajamas, said quickly, "Okay, Gerry, I'll go with you. But I have to use the toilet first." She walked straight ahead and Gerry had to step aside to let her pass.

"Brilliant," Gerry said, his voice an angry whisper. "Why don't you give her my address while you're at it?"

"I'm sorry, I made a mistake."

"You're sorry all right."

"Hey, this wasn't my stupid idea."

"What's so stupid, she's coming with us?"

Timmy realized, then, the part of the plan they'd forgotten. "Coming with us where? Where are we taking her?" Gerry stood rigid for a second, then his shoulders slumped.

The toilet flushed. They listened to the water run in the sink. The mayor re-entered the room, smiling. "It's all taken care of, boys." She crossed the rug with the smooth insistence of a great boat floating from one river bank to the other, backed onto the cushions as if she were berthing at a pier. "You know why you don't have jobs, don't you?" She lifted another cookie. "Because you're dumb as goats. Don't you ever watch TV? The first rule of kidnapping is never let a hostage out of your sight. I just called the chief of police from the phone in the bathroom. They'll be here in two minutes."

"Shit," Gerry said, pausing long enough to give Timmy an accusatory look before dashing for the door. He threw it open, stepped into the hallway, and looked back. "Let's go."

Timmy stood in the middle of the room. It felt like everything that had happened to him the last few years had collapsed upon him. The thought of being arrested filled him less with fear, than a sense of relief. At least in jail, it would be over. He wouldn't have to worry, or think. And he wouldn't have to pretend any more that he hadn't become what he was—a failure. There'd be no more denying it. Everyone would know. "Thank you," he said to the mayor, and he removed his mask.

"What are you doing?" Gerry was incredulous. He looked frantically up and down the hallway.

"Go. I won't squeal. But I can't take no more nothing."

The mayor's mouth hung open in surprise. From the doorway, Gerry raised his fists and shook them. Then he was gone.

"My life is a mess," Timmy said, and he started to cry. He stood in the middle of the room feeling more alone than he could ever remember. He couldn't even lift his hands to wipe his face.

For almost an hour, Timmy spoke about the fears and pressures and uncertainties of his life. About how worthless he felt, how useless, unable to bring anything of value into his home. He talked about how he had no one to rely on, not people, not God, and then he got into the whole subject of Katie, her illness, and his inability to do even the slightest thing to help. The mayor encouraged him to sit beside her. She put her arm around his shoulders and he curled into her touch. "I want her to be my girl again," he said, "and have like, something to look forward to, possibilities. Going out on dates and me getting nervous, waiting. You know? Having picnics, or taking in a movie, anything. I just want her life to be good."

"Life isn't good only when it's pleasant," the mayor said, and she gave his shoulders a squeeze.

"I don't even know what to want for her. I don't know what it's even possible to wish for." Timmy sat up, rubbing at his eyes. He felt like a fool. Looking at the door, he said, to change the subject, "Jeez, the cops are slow."

She laughed. "You watch too much TV. Why would there be a phone in the bathroom? This is Pittsburgh, not Los Angeles."

She passed him one of the scraped-clean oreo wafers. He gulped it down, surprised to find himself famished.

"I get so tired of fighting all the time," he told her. "Fighting with the unemployment, fighting with the insurance, the disability people. Every month me and Pat sit down and spend a whole night writing letters to politicians. Nobody ever does nothing. I even tried to get some money from the union emergency fund, but..."

"You put too much trust in the wrong things," she interrupted. "Unions, governments, churches—those are just horrible institutions. They're rotten through and through. They don't have hearts. They don't feel anything. What makes Pittsburgh Pittsburgh are its people. If you want help, look around your neighborhood. You grew up here, you must have friends."

Timmy thought about that. About Jim, and the volunteers, and the owner of Veltre's, and the print shop where they ran off the posters. Even Gerry was trying to help. "You're right," he said. "But it's just so hard sometimes..."

"Everything's hard that's worth doing. Listen. When I was a kid, we lived at the bottom of Murray Ave. We had to walk up the hill to do the shopping, the laundry, everything. Oh, did I complain. Finally, one day my mother says to me—I must've been about ten—she says, All this complaining from such a little girl who every day has two parents to come home to. This life, it all the time goes up the hill. But at least it goes." Her eyes lost a bit of their shine as she stared down at her feet, moving her slippers back and forth so the toes touched, came apart. "You're blessed with a family. Would you rather they were all dead?"

"No," Timmy said. He felt a coldness pass through him.

"The only thing your kids really need is you."

"That's easy for you to say, you have a job," he said.

She inclined her head, granting him the point. "Tell you what. You want a job? If I remember, the city just received Federal money for the Parks Department, to hire single mothers. I can get you in there."

Timmy looked at her. He ran his tongue along his teeth to

clean off the cookie grit. "I'm a guy," he said.

"You'd be surprised at some of the 'single mothers' we find when we're getting federal funds. It's all paperwork hon. Nobody checks up. All they're looking for is numbers on a sheet. We can make you look like you come from Swahili if we need to."

Timmy looked at his hands, opened in his lap, the crosshatched lines of his empty palms. He remembered the way it used to feel when the cashier counted the smooth, dry bills into his hand on payday; then how he'd repeat that ritual at home, passing the bills over to Pat. The thought of getting a regular check again—Could it really be this easy? Then he told himself, single mother. He remembered the woman giving massages. And how many others just like her? Sure, he didn't feel it was right to reserve jobs just for women, and certainly he needed the work as much as anyone. But still, it wasn't right to take a job meant for someone else. Why did he have to be put in the position of taking someone else's work? If he did this, wouldn't he be the same as a scab? "I can't do it," he said. "I can't take something meant for someone else. I got to live with myself, too."

She made a *pshaw* sound, like he was being stupid. "If you don't take it, some councilor's son or daughter or cousin will. It's not going to go to any single mother." She looked closely at his face. "In your father's day, if he didn't have family in the union, he had to buy a union card. You wanted to be a cop, you paid your ward chairman. I could go out tomorrow and get a $1500 campaign donation for this job." There was an emotionless, uncompromising quality to her eyes, a growing sense of impatience in the set of her mouth. "That's how it works."

"That's the problem," Timmy said.

"Do you want it?" she asked. "Or not?"

Was that what it was all about? Wasn't anything else important? What about doing things because they were the right thing to do? He shook his head. "I'm not going to screw over other people who are just as bad off as me."

She walked him out of the apartment into the hallway.

"Remember," she told him, retreating back inside, pulling the door nearly closed until only one of her eyes, half her smile, the side view of her nose, were visible. "I could still call and have you arrested. I know your name, where you live." Timmy held his breath, his mouth sagged into an oval of fear. "But I won't." He exhaled and drew in a deep breath. "I'm doing you a favor," she said and her finger, visible in the crack of the door, rose slowly until it was parallel with her nose. "Remember though, I'll be needing some help in your neighborhood when re-election time comes around."

He stood on the corner by the phone booth in a cold, misting rain. He felt weak, dizzy, as if he might collapse. No way did he have the energy to walk home. Forget the money for a cab. The notion of trying to figure out bus routes and schedules overwhelmed him. He felt hollowed inside, sucked dry by exhaustion, much the way he used to feel after working a double shift at the plant in 90 degree heat in the summer.

I got to do something, he thought as he lifted the receiver. Water was beaded on the black plastic. He tried to wipe it dry on his coat, but only succeeded in smearing the beads into short dashes. I don't care if Pat screams at me all night, he told himself. Even as he thought that, though, he knew she'd never scream at him all night. Her anger was like flash paper. It burned and disappeared without leaving any residue. How could he even think she'd hold onto it to torment him? Was he trying to pretend she was a harsh person, just so he could feel sorry for himself? Set her up as some kind of villainess, which she wasn't? He thought back to what it had been like when they were young, courting. Their easy banter and joy in one another; the excitement and wonder of finding where to touch to cause each other pleasure, make each other laugh. The discovery, too, of those sad places which needed a different kind of touch, something not so defined, so they could be healed.

Courting, he thought. What a crazy word. Then he saw it clearly, as if a movie were unreeling before him, what it was he needed to do. What they needed to do for each other.

The rain had matted his hair and jacket, was actually running off his nose in a steady stream. He plugged a quarter into the slot and dialed the one person he knew could help him get home.

But when Timmy heard Jim's familiar, "Yup?" Timmy didn't know what to say. His mouth was dry and he tried to work some saliva up by squishing his jaws together. He ran his tongue over his lips, then pulled his lips inside his mouth and sucked on them. He recognized a giddiness in his head, a mixture of fear and euphoria like the kind he'd experienced back when he started dating Pat, and had to write down a list of topics to discuss, questions to ask, so he wouldn't run out of things to say to her when they talked on the phone.

"Yello—is anybody there?" Jim called, drawing out the last word and giving it an upwards lilt.

Timmy looked back at the tall brick building he'd just come from. Most of the lights were out and it looked like nothing so much as a large, rectangular storage box. Across the street, the Food Gallery lot was empty. The orange neon of the sign made the store's name appear to float and hover in the air. The three pairs of streetlights reflected hazy, overlapping circles on the road, the light diffusing on the tar in a way that made it impossible to determine where the edges of the reflections were.

"Last chance," Jim said. In the background, Timmy heard children laughing. For one, unsettled second he thought the laughing girl was Katie.

"Hey buddy," Timmy managed to stammer. He was afraid Jim wouldn't recognize his voice.

"You little weiner. Don't you know obscene calls are supposed to start with heavy breathing? The silence comes later."

Timmy gave a little laugh and Jim chuckled, the sound so comforting Timmy stood and listened to it without feeling the need to say anything.

"Well, you're the big topic of discussion," Jim said.

"What do you mean?" Timmy felt the cold again, the rain,

and he hunched close to the phone, wishing that they had never done away with the booths which had at least offered some small protection.

"I mean Ellen's over here, Shirley's over your house, and nobody knows where you are."

It was all a little too complicated for Timmy to sort through at that moment. "My car broke down," he said.

"Where?"

"Over Gerry's."

"Is he gonna give you a ride back?"

"I'm in Shadyside," Timmy said.

"Okay." Jim paused. "Is this twenty questions? You want me to guess?" Jim asked, his voice cast in that slight, bobbing tone he used when he was teasing.

Timmy turned towards the street, his face breaking into a smile as he told Jim, "We were gonna kidnap the mayor."

Jim laughed.

"And ransom her for jobs."

Jim laughed harder.

"And then she offered me work as a single mother."

Jim gave out a hooting guffaw. "Did I tell you the Steelers want me to play quarterback?"

They laughed with each other for a few seconds, then Jim told Timmy, "Hold the gory details until I get there. Now give me your co-ordinates."

Timmy was standing, shivering, his mind blank, when he heard a loud, guttering engine. He looked up from the sidewalk to see headlights angled right at him. The car didn't appear to be slowing, looked like it would jump the curb. Timmy took a step back, hesitating over which way to move, when the car straightened at the last moment. The brakes squealed, and the front end bobbed down, then back up as it came to a halt. Jim flung his door open, jumped out and said, "Chinese fire drill." Timmy watched Jim run once around the car and hunker in the passenger's side. "Hey," Jim yelled as he rolled down the window and stuck his head out into the rain. "I don't care about you, but my car seats are getting soaked." Timmy shook his head. Only in Pittsburgh, he thought. He banged his hand on the hood and hopped into the street, headed for the driver's door. He ducked inside, moved the seat forward, and adjusted the mirror. He got himself all set, ready to go, then he snapped on his left blinker and turned to Jim.

"Tell me everything," Jim told him. "I want to hear it all. I want to see the photos. I want to smell the farts."

Timmy laughed. Then he looked at Jim, at the stitches running like a crooked, black stick across his forehead.

Jim touched at his wound. "Yeah, the bastards tried to lobotomize me, but it wouldn't work."

"Nothing to lobotomize?" Timmy said. Jim punched him in the arm, then grabbed his forearm and gave it a shake. They looked at each other. Jim's eyes held their humor, but took on a probing quality. "So. What's going on buddy?" Jim asked.

"I'll tell you," Timmy said. After first checking behind him, he pulled into the road.

When he spoke, Timmy didn't feel like he was telling a story. It had more of the sensation of a revelation. It was like he'd opened up his body to reveal everything inside; his ribcage, his lungs, his internal organs; the bright, red, glistening globe of his ever-beating heart. And when he looked over, Jim was watching, listening, his face full of concern and a strange glow, like bliss.

Chapter 18

AFTER SHE HUNG UP from talking to Jim, Shirley came back and stood by the couch. She lifted her can of Iron City and finished it off in a few swallows. "You know," she said. "We got the hardest jobs in the world. We got to take care of our kids. We got to take care of our husbands. Then we got to take care of this...thing...this family thing. We got to take care of everyone's needs one by one, then the needs we have all together. It's like that U-2 song..." She started humming in a strong, low voice that was flat but sounded okay. "You know, the one about how you give, and give, until you give yourself away."

I tried to sing along, but I always had a voice like a frog croaking.

"Great harmony," Shirley said, and we laughed. She pointed her finger at me. "But ain't that the truth?" She crushed her can flat between her hands and tossed it atop the other three flattened cans on the coffee table. "But I wouldn't want to work in no office, or on some assembly line, because when you do pull it all together..." She shook her head, her smile seeming to come from far, far away. I knew exactly what she meant.

"It's people like us who keep this whole thing going," I said. "All this other crap is just bullshit. We're the ones who run the show. But we never get any credit for nothing. I mean, you read in the papers about women lawyers, and business this and that—don't we count?"

Shirley set one hand on her hip and shifted her weight

165

from side to side, shaking her hips in rhythmn as she spoke. "Honey they got money and we talk funny." I laughed.

"But ain't that the shit, though?" She took one last drag of her cigarette and ground it out. She stood, her nose in the air, and announced like she was some society matron, "You ladies simply aren't classy enough." She drew out the *A* in classy. "But we know better. Anyways, I gotta go."

That's when she told me about the phone call. She had to get back because Jim was going to pick up Timmy. My first reaction was, "Don't leave me."

She took my face in both her hands and gave me a hard kiss on the forehead.

"There are some things even I don't stick my nose in." She paused at the door and winked. "Just get on your Frederick's of Hollywood stuff."

"You mean the lacy pumpkin outfit?" I said, trying to joke, but God I was nervous.

"Yeah, that's the ticket. Your edible underwear," she said. "The kielbasa and kraut flavor."

I laughed a little harder than I should've, trying to keep her there. But she was gone.

I had to wait a long time. In one way, I was glad. In another—I just wanted to get it over with. Get what over with, I didn't know. But something had to give. Having spent the whole night worrying about what was going on with him and not knowing for the first time—not having the faintest clue what was running through his head...I mean, in the past we could read each other like books. When had that stopped? And why? And what could I do about it? Something had changed between us, and I knew, as I sat there waiting, thinking, listening to the clock tick, something had to change again. I had to change. He had to. We both had to. But I didn't have an idea in hell what that meant.

Around eleven, he pulled up in our car, Jim right behind him. I watched the two guys hug in the middle of the street and thought, Timmy must've been drinking. But when he stepped inside the door, I didn't smell any alcohol. I looked at him and he stood there, just inside the doorway, like he wanted to tell me something real important. Only he said, "The car's fixed. Jim did it tonight."

"I saw you pull up," I said. I could hear in his voice how happy he was. He had that same tone Ellen and Katie used to have when they were little, and had just discovered something—an ant, the name for a color—for the first time. Like learning something was the greatest thing that could happen to you.

"In this weather?" I asked. He nodded. "Great," I told him. I looked at his face; lips, nose, the stubble on his cheeks, his thick eyebrows. But I couldn't bring myself to look into his eyes even though he kept lowering his face, as if that's what he needed me to do. Look at him so I could see something. I was trying to be nice, but I was so nervous. I don't know why. But the two of us, just standing there, finally I told him, "I haven't been out of the house all night. I need to get some air."

I guess because he was standing in front of the door, and I didn't want to push around him, I turned and walked out the back way. I looked over at the bulkhead, a dark, threatening form at night. My knee was aching and the back of my neck started to throb. The rain had slowed down, and it wasn't much more than a heavy wetness in the air. It wasn't so much falling, as just there; not something that happened to you, but something you had to live with. I looked at our small yard and remembered Katie sitting in the snow in her snowsuit, while I stood inside thinking she was being bad. You know God, I thought, I thank you for all these volunteers, and for Ellen and Timmy, and Shirley and Jim—they're all blessings. But sometimes...sometimes I don't know where You are. I know You're there somewhere, but I don't know where. I don't know what You're doing. Maybe that's the point. Maybe we're the ones who are supposed to be doing. But what?

I walked out to the alley running behind our building, then around the front to our street. Across the way, the lights were on in Shirley's bedroom, and I could hear her hard laughter, joining with Jim's. Our front door was open. I went inside.

Timmy was in the upstairs bathroom. I wanted to go to him. Instead, I sat on the couch until I heard him finish peeing in the toilet (he didn't flush it, waiting for me to use it first so we could save on the water and the noise.) It was always the last thing he did before going to bed. I knew it was safe now. I could take my bath first, before I had to talk to him.

For some reason, sitting in the water, my legs floating, I got scared. It was like someone was folding a dark blanket over my face. I couldn't breathe and my heart started pounding. I pushed myself up and stood, dripping, on the floor mat.

In the full-length mirror on the inside of the bathroom door, my reflection made me miserable. Not just the weight. My shoulders were heavy and stooped, my breasts sagged, and there was that low slung belt of flesh on my belly. All those things men, I guess, would notice. For me, the other things were worse; the flecks of gray dotting my pubic hair, the sickly, yellow tone to my skin and, especially, my face.

The brown rims sunken in the skin beneath my eyes seemed permanent. My mouth looked like it had been gouged in, a downward slanting line, as if I never smiled. There were more streaks of gray in my hair than in Timmy's. Why had I never noticed that? I thought, My God, we're both barely past thirty. How did we get so old?

From the end of the hallway, where the stairs emptied at Katie's bedroom, I heard a moan. I grabbed my bathrobe off the top of the hamper and slipped it on as I ran towards the sound. I flicked on the hallway light, pushed her door open. I could see the makeshift wooden bars Timmy had nailed together for her, for this girl, this young lady now, my daughter. Stepping closer, I saw that she was relaxed on the mattress, her face beaming like it does after a startle-reaction. What if she didn't get better? Would that be terrible for her? I wiped at my eyes with my fingertips. What if she was happier this way? They say ignorance is bliss. How could I possibly know what was best, for anyone? But wasn't that my job? Wasn't I supposed to find out?

She smiled and I said, "Honey, I can't do anything more for you today. I've got nothing left to give." I brushed her hair back with my fingers and kissed her forehead. "See you tomorrow."

I backed out of her room and turned towards our bedroom, Timmy's and mine. He had a right to know what was going on. But as I drew closer to the door, I felt almost as terrified as I had the day I found Katie unconscious, that fear of not knowing what had happened, or what would come to pass, only knowing things were going to change.

He was sitting up against the headboard, wearing his Star Wars pajamas. Space ships battled on his chest in a sky of dark blue. His hands were clasped behind his head; his arms made triangles pointing at opposite walls. When I stepped in, his face was calm with a cautious hope.

I stopped at the end of the bed and looked down at the hill formed by his feet, the slope of the white bedspread. The shadows of the folds were a cold blue and I shivered. I thought of Ellen, today at the lunch, the way I'd zoomed bread at her mouth. The way she'd fed me, I'd fed her. Shirley coming over when I needed to talk. I knew me and Timmy, we should do something for each other. Still, I couldn't move.

"Pat?" Timmy said gently.

"I'm just trying to have faith that everything will work out," I said. At first I thought that was a stupid thing to say—what did it have to do with anything? But he told me, "Me too." He moved his feet up. The hill disappeared and a larger mountain of white grew as his knees lifted.

He said, "But we can't expect things to go back to the way they were before. We just have to have faith that we can take what comes along and get through it." He pulled the blanket from the empty space to his left and patted the mattress. "C'mere. I been thinking a lot tonight. I got a new program," he said. "This one's for us."

I joined him. But as he put his left arm behind me, I tensed up. He pulled me closer anyways. When I lay my head on his chest, it felt like I was bumping into something solid. I pushed away.

"It's okay. We can touch each other. We're not carriers," he said.

I shut my eyes and tried to relax. He rested his chin on my head and ran his hand lightly over my back, his fingers barely touching the terry cloth of my robe. "Now, let me show you," he said. "I got this all thought out."

"You? Thinking?" I said.

His moustache straightened as he smiled. "Hard to believe, ain't it?" he said. "Now." He placed my left hand inside his pajama tops. I idly stroked the hairs running down the middle of his chest. "That's the good girl," he joked. "See? It's not so hard." He slipped his right hand inside my robe, placing it on my left side, just below my breast. "We start here," he said. "Rub for a count of five, then move to a new place."

"Like musical chairs?" I said.

"Or fire drill with your hands. You ready?"

I squeezed his side, tickling him. He squirmed and laughed. "Quit it. I didn't say Go yet," he told me.

I held my hand up in innocence. "Sorry. This is new to me. Anyways, you didn't really explain it too good."

He closed his mouth, still grinning, and ran his tongue over his teeth. "All right. I'll show you."

He replaced his hand on my side with an exaggerated motion. I slapped my hand onto his chest so hard it made a hollow thump. He gave a jerk, pretended I'd knocked the breath out of him. "Oh quit it, you big baby," I said. His eyes were lively, alert, focused entirely on me. It gave me this feeling like everything inside my skin had turned liquid. My eyes started watering and I shut them quick. "Let's get this show on the road," I said.

"Okay," Timmy said. "You count. I'll move.

"One, two, three, four, five..." I said.

He moved first his hand, then mine, from place to place on our bodies in a parody of lovers' touches. I counted faster, slurring the words together. He moved our hands frantically, trying to keep up; from our sides, to our fronts, to our faces, to our backs. He was close, but always just missed getting them where they were supposed to be.

Soon we were both counting, both moving our arms. We began poking each other, and started laughing. Our arms became entangled. We laughed so hard we couldn't do anything but fall forward and cling together. The laughter wound down, came out in gasps, and we settled lower on the mattress.

On our sides, face to face, we began in earnest. Our caresses were tight at first, our fingers and lips stiff as we grasped and lunged at each other. But our bodies were intent, eager, and we quickly learned the rhythmn of it. Our mouths and hands began to move on their own. It was like instinct. Only not exactly.

For me, it was like rediscovering something I'd forgotten, creating a new, yet familiar, pattern. My lips and hands rushed and blundered, urgent and awkward. It was as if my mouth and tongue had found, again, the joy of those early babbling sounds, as if my touches were the first, gleeful, tottering steps of a baby learning how to walk.

"Oh, Timmy," I said, and he knew what I meant. When he penetrated me, I could feel an opening out and a closing in, a pulling together, a connection with everything outside ourselves, and a force as pure and strong as light rushing in to join us.

Epilogue

I'M NOT GOING to lie. I'm not going to say that things are easy now, or even that they're good. They're better. There's hope. For all of us. But it's still hard.

Katie will be eighteen this May and it breaks my heart. But we're in a new program, something one of the new volunteers told me about. Run by doctors down at this Institute in Philly. We like it a lot, me and Timmy; these people have helped us, not went against us, but oh God, it's hard. They don't want to hear no ands, ifs, or buts. I mean, we're supposed to do 600 forward and backward rolls a day with her. One hundred walks up the incline plane. Twenty patternings. I had to make seventy-five cards with pictures, and the words for the pictures on the back—they're making me into a reading teacher. I mean, I've never read a book in my life! We're doing addition, subtraction, all that stuff that didn't seem important to me when I was in school. Back then, I didn't really see the point in learning nothing. What would I use it for? Girls, you know, in my time, in Pittsburgh, all you needed to know was how to run a house. Of course, back then I didn't have a clue what that meant, how difficult it was. I swear, sometimes I think you've got to be either an Einstein or an idiot to hold it together.

Anyways, we give Katie oxygen five times a day, have to put her in this spacesuit and lay her on her stomach, hooked up to a respiratory machine Timmy made from an old vacuum cleaner, to help her breathe deeper. It gets more oxygen to her brain. That's what they told us, down the clinic. These people in Philly, they're a gift from God, they really are. They love Katie. But they don't listen when you tell them it's real hard to find the volunteers.

"What do you want, sympathy?" my advocate said to me. She's a sweet young woman from Guatemala. "We don't have much time," she said. "Katie's getting older. Think of it like, she's someone caught up in her body and you have to get her out of there."

"Yeah, I know the feeling, too," I said to the girl, but she didn't really laugh. She was too young to know.

I've got a brace on my knee, and I have to have it drained sometimes, and they think I might have a herniated disc in my neck, but I'm still fighting. Writing to congressmen, arguing with social security, putting flyers up; God, I been everywhere. Sometimes I feel like I've got to hassle with people just to breathe. But, you know, this is the life I've got, what else can I do with it?

Timmy's okay. He and Jim had a good little business for themselves for a while, all under the table. They made signs, GOING OUT OF BUSINESS, FOR SALE. There was a big boom for a while, and we were able to pick up a few extra things, but once everything closed up there was no one left to sell to. He finally got work at the new mall, scooping ice cream. After just one year they made him assistant manager, and it wasn't so embarrassing anymore. We can laugh now about him having to wear white pants and shirts. He calls himself the Guardian Angel of vanilla. The pay's crap, but at least we never have to buy milk.

And Ellen, Lord help us—she's taking sex education this year and I told her, "If you start using some of that stuff, I'll break your neck." I almost freaked when I thought I saw a hickey on her shoulder, but it turned out to be just a bruise.

Still, you know, there's something strange about it all, this whole way we're living. It feels like it's not finished or something. I been thinking lately a lot about what does God want me to do with my life. "Just live it," Timmy said when I told him, and maybe he's right. But sometimes things happen and I don't know what they mean, or if I'll ever know, or whether I should try to figure them out or just go on. Like today...

I was driving down to Zayre's to get some stocking stuffers for Ellen and Katie. There'd been a light dusting of snow during the night. It had melted about noon, then froze as the sky thickened with a low, gray ceiling of clouds and the temperature dropped twenty degrees. When I went out, it was late afternoon. The sun was like this huge orange ball that had broken apart and was spilling all over the horizon. It caught the ice on the road and the glare was so bright, I could barely see. I was afraid of getting in an accident. Traffic was stop-and-go and I rode on the bumper of the car before me.

As I took a right out of the back street of row houses, headed past another closed-up plant, drove under the railroad trestle and came to the access road running alongside Zayre's parking lot, a thick, fluttery feeling started up in my chest. I looked past the car in front of me, down the road. The orange glare of the ice turned the street, and its shoulder, into a surface of flames. There, standing in the flames fifty feet ahead, I saw Katie. She was on the side of the road, holding something in her hands, cupping it, so that her fingers glowed. It was brighter than fire, and I shook my head, trying to clear it. But she was still there.

She was smiling, her mouth moving, trying to tell me something, but I couldn't hear, I couldn't understand. "What?" I said. "What is it?" She kept trying to tell me, but I couldn't make it out.

Her eyes took on this sparkle. I could see her so clearly, standing there, her hands glowing, her eyes shining like two miniature suns brought down to earth. I couldn't see anything else but her. But I couldn't understand what she needed. I had to pull over, I was crying so hard.

And when I stopped, she was gone.